Reaping Trouble

As he and the others walked back toward the house, Chet pointed out the numerous small ponds dotting the pastures to the east, as well as some old stone walls and copses of trees. "The farm was a great place to play when we were younger," he concluded. "Lots of hiding places, for hide-and-seek."

"Plenty of places to lurk around, too—if you're intent on causing trouble," Frank noted.

The others nodded their agreement, and they all walked around the barn toward the rear of the house.

As they passed the barn doors, a loud roar sounded from inside. Without warning, both doors burst open and a huge tractor barreled out, heading straight toward them.

The Hardy Boys Mystery Stories

Available from ALADDIN Paperbacks

THE HARDY BOYS®

#188
FARMING FEAR

FRANKLIN W. DIXON

Aladdin Paperbacks
New York London Toronto Sydney

First Aladdin Paperbacks edition December 2004
Copyright © 2004 by Simon & Schuster, Inc.

ALADDIN PAPERBACKS
An imprint of Simon & Schuster
Children's Publishing Division
1230 Avenue of the Americas
New York, NY 10020

The text of this book was set in New Caledonia.

Printed in the United States of America
2 4 6 8 10 9 7 5 3 1

Library of Congress Control Number 2004102694

ISBN 0-689-86739-5

Contents

1 Trouble on the Old Homestead

"We're worried about our grandparents," Iola Morton said as she sat next to Joe Hardy on the big couch in the Hardys' living room.

Her brother, Chet, sitting in a lounger near the TV, nodded in agreement. "They're having trouble with the family farm," he said. "Iola and I aren't really sure what to do."

"What kind of trouble?" Joe Hardy asked, putting his arm around Iola's shoulder.

Iola looked anxiously from her boyfriend to his brother, Frank, who was seated on the opposite end of the couch. "Well, a lot of the farm's equipment has broken down very recently," she began. "The animals are acting spooked, and shadowy figures have been lurking around the woods at the edge of the property."

"Not only that," Chet continued, "but stuff has been disappearing. Small tools and things, mostly—right out in the barn!"

"You're thinking theft?" Joe said.

Chet nodded. "Our grandparents have contacted the police, but . . ."

"But what?" Frank asked.

"You know how the cops can be," Chet said. "They think our grandparents are just farmers worrying about winter and becoming forgetful in their old age."

"That's not true, though," Iola interjected. "Our grandparents are just as sharp as they ever were."

"Yeah," Chet agreed. "You don't ever want to play my granddad at chess."

"I did once," Joe said, "that summer we went to your family picnic, four years ago. Your grandpa Dave cleaned my clock!"

"And Grandma Marge is a wiz at Chinese checkers, not to mention crossword puzzles," Iola added, "so we know they're not losing their marbles."

"What do your parents think about all this?" Frank asked, his brown eyes gleaming. "Have they seen any of these intruders on the farm?"

"Our folks are away on a cruise," Iola said. "They won't be back for weeks."

Frank slapped his forehead. "I'd forgotten that,"

he said. The dark-haired eighteen-year-old glanced at his younger brother. Joe nodded back. They knew they had to help their friends.

"Our parents are lounging on some secluded Caribbean island," Chet said. "It's the first vacation they've had in years."

"Grandpa and Grandma don't want us to get involved," Iola added. "They insist they can handle this themselves, but . . ."

"But you're not so sure," Joe said.

Iola nodded.

"So you want our help," Frank concluded.

"Sure," Chet said. "You guys have solved piles of cases before the police even stumbled out of their squad cars."

"Con Riley or Officer Sullivan might dispute that," Frank noted, chuckling.

Iola took a deep breath. "The farm has been in our family for over five generations," she said. "Even the barn dates back to 1927. Our grandparents have lived in their house since Bayport was a tiny seaside village. They love that farm. It would break their hearts to give it up! But they can't handle this trouble on their own, and they're too proud to ask for help."

"So Iola and I were planning on spending our winter break there, helping out," Chet said.

"Most of their workers go south when it gets cold," Iola explained. "Chet and I have already asked if you two could come and stay with us over

3

vacation, and our grandparents said yes—assuming you want to."

"Of course we'll help," Joe said. He gave his girlfriend a reassuring hug.

"We asked Callie, too," Chet said, "but she's gone skiing with her family."

"Yeah, I know," Frank said, a little sadly. Callie Shaw was Frank's girlfriend, and she often joined the group on adventures like this. "How soon do we leave?" Frank asked.

"Just as soon as you're packed," Chet replied.

An hour and a half later, the Hardys' van rolled down the long driveway of the Morton Farm. The farm lay northwest of Bayport, beyond the interstate. Strip malls, subdivisions, and other developments crept farther west every year, but they hadn't reached this part of town yet. It was still very quiet. The gently rolling landscape made the Morton farm especially beautiful in the winter. Snowfall from recent storms covered the property in a blanket of pure white. Sunlight glistened off low drifts and ice-covered tree branches.

The Morton's driveway approached the white farmhouse from the south. A big red barn and several wooden sheds stood in the back yard. A huge pasture stretched from behind the barn to a thick evergreen forest on the north property line. High-power electrical transmission lines towered over the woods. Another white farmhouse sat on top of a forested hill beyond the metal-ribbed titans.

To the west, the Mortons' fields stretched all the way out to Kendall Ridge Road. A line of bare, snow-covered trees separated the property from the street. The road wound up the hill to the adjoining farmlands beyond.

To the east, the tilled fields gave way to wild pasture dotted with slender evergreens. The Hardys remembered horses and cows grazing in that part of the farm during the summer. A wide stand of tall pine trees, which joined the forest on the north, sprang up at the far eastern edge of the pasture.

The Morton farmhouse was a proud structure, dating back to the beginning of the twentieth century. It stood two stories tall with a huge central chimney and several pointed roofs. Shuttered windows peeked out from beneath the roof's icy brows. A wide, covered veranda ran around the front of the house. A shoveled walk stretched from the porch to the driveway.

The drive curved around to the house's rear and looped around. The barn stood on the far side of the driveway about twenty yards away from the Mortons' back door. Both the barn and the house looked as though they could use a good coat of paint, as did the doghouse sitting near the back path. Beside the barn stood several old wooden sheds and an insulated, metal water tower. The rusty tower, which was nearly as tall as the barn, rested on four stout, wooden posts. A circular, wooden, pointed roof crowned its top, and a spigot, electric pump system, and big storage box occupied the space beneath.

Joe parked the van near the drive that led up to the back door. All four teens piled out and got their luggage.

"I really love this place," Iola said, sighing wistfully.

"We have a lot of great memories here," Chet agreed.

"Who owns the house at the top of that hill?" Frank asked.

"J. J. Zuis," Chet replied, "an old family friend."

"Zeus?" Frank asked. "Like the Greek god?"

"Z-U-I-S," Iola said, spelling it out. "It's pronounced 'zoo-iss.' A Lithuanian name, I think."

"So," Joe said looking around, "Mr. Zuis is an old family friend—and are there any old family enemies?"

Chet and Iola glanced at each other and chimed, "The Costellos."

"What's the problem with the Costellos?" Frank asked.

"The old man's not very neighborly," Chet replied.

"And the son is a creep!" Iola added.

"Now, now," said a gruff voice, "I won't have you kids badmouthin' the neighbors."

Dave Morton, dressed in overalls, a blue parka, and a red knit hat, sauntered out the back door to meet them. White clouds of frost bloomed from Grandpa Morton's mouth as he spoke. The wind tugged at his white hair where it slipped out from under his cap, and his gray eyes twinkled. "You kids may not think much of the Costellos, and maybe I don't either," he said, "but Grandma and I still have to live next to 'em."

He smiled and threw open his arms. "Come give your old gramps a big hug." Chet and Iola ran up to him. "You must be Frank and Joe," he said, shaking hands with the brothers. "You've gotten big since I last saw you!"

"Good to see you," Frank said.

"Come inside before you freeze," Grandpa replied. He motioned them all through the back door. They took their winter gear off in the mudroom, then they went into the kitchen. The smell of fresh-baked cookies greeted them as they entered. A broad grin broke over Chet's round face.

"She knew you were coming," Grandpa Morton noted wryly.

A short, stout woman with white hair turned from the old-fashioned gas stove to face the group. Her gray eyes narrowed playfully behind her wire-rim glasses. "Now, Pa, I won't have either you or Chet snatching any of these cookies off the rack while they're cooling."

"Your grandmother knows you like a book, Chet," Frank said.

Grandpa Morton chuckled. "Marge, you remember the Hardy boys—Frank and Joe?"

"Joe's the blond, right?" Grandma Morton asked. She gazed appraisingly at the seventeen-year-old. "I've been hearing a lot about you, young man."

"All of it good, I hope," Joe replied, his blue eyes twinkling.

Grandma shrugged and smiled back. "Sure, some of it," she said with a laugh. "We've got all your rooms ready. Joe and Frank, you'll be sharin' one on the second floor. I hope you don't mind bunks. Chet's in the room next to yours, and Iola is in the guest bed on the main level."

"Those are the rooms we usually stay in during the summer," Iola explained.

"Bunk beds are fine by us," Frank said.

"Dibs on the top!" Joe said.

"You can throw your things in your rooms and then join us for some milk and cookies," Mrs. Morton said.

It took about fifteen minutes for the teenagers to get their unpacking squared away, then another twenty to enjoy Grandma's fresh-baked cookies with milk. While the teens ate, the Morton grandparents quickly got back to their chores.

"Do your grandparents know we're here to find the cause of the . . . trouble?" Frank asked.

Chet and Iola shook their heads. "No," Iola said.

"We thought about telling them," Chet added, "but then they might not have agreed to let you come."

Frank nodded. "I understand them not wanting outside help, but if the police won't step in—"

"If we're going to crack this case," Joe interrupted, "I think we should probably start with a tour of the farm." He and the others bused their dishes to the sink, and then bundled up and went outside again.

The sky had clouded over since their arrival, and snow flurries punctuated the chilly air.

"Let's start with the barn," Chet said, leading them toward the big, red, wooden structure. "There's a storage and work area in the front of the barn; the horse stalls and cow pens are kept in a separate, heated extension in the back."

"I didn't think your grandparents did any dairy work," Joe said.

"They have a couple of cows for fresh milk," Iola replied. "It may not make economic sense, but it's kind of a tradition."

"They have the horses for tradition, too," Chet

9

said. "The animals connect them to their youth, before farm work became so mechanized."

"And it's nice that us grandkids can go riding when we visit," Iola finished.

As the teens talked, Chet slid back the bolt and opened the barn's tall double doors. As the portal swung open, a gray-and-white blur flashed out at them. A huge English sheepdog landed on Chet's chest, knocking him onto his back.

"Down, Bernie! Down!" Chet said as the dog licked his face. "We're glad to see you, too."

Bernie bounded off of Chet and circled Iola and the Hardys, kicking up small clouds of powdery snow in his wake and barking happily.

The brothers laughed and patted the dog on the head.

"You've got to watch out for Bernie," Iola warned. "Sometimes his enthusiasm gets out of hand. Bernie, heel!" The big, shaggy dog stopped circling and sat beside her.

Chet rose and dusted himself off, then all four teens and Bernie went into the barn and shut the door behind them. The interior of the barn was one big room. A hayloft circled the building's high ceiling. Numerous storage stalls lined the walls, and straw covered the bare dirt floor.

A doorway on the far wall led to the horse and cow enclosure. A big, green tractor with a toolbox next to it stood in the middle of the room's floor.

Harness and tack for the horses were stowed in a stall to the right of the main doors. To the left, a big sheet covered an object the size of a small car.

"You'll love this," Chet said, pulling the burlap off with a flourish. Underneath rested something that looked like a huge go-cart. It had two seats in front, a bench seat behind, four fat wheels, and an engine all the way in the back. The machine's body consisted entirely of metal frame—it had no side panels or roof. A padded roll cage ran above the passenger compartment. Bare headlights—like bugged-out eyes—stuck out on top of the vehicle's front bumper.

Joe scratched his blond head. "Um . . . what is it?"

"It's the chassis from an old VW Beetle, right?" Frank said.

"Give the man a prize!" Iola replied.

"Okay, but what's it for?" Joe asked.

"It's for tooling around the farm," Chet explained. "During the work season, the farmhands use it to get to and from the fields. We call it 'the buggy.'"

"It's not street legal, though," Frank noted.

"We only run it on our own property," Iola replied. "That way it doesn't need a license. It's sort of a stripped-down dune buggy."

"Goes great in the snow, too," Chet added, "kind of like a big four-wheeler. Maybe we can run around in it later."

"Sounds fun," Joe said.

The four of them finished the tour of the barn, stopping to meet the horses and cows, and then they went out back to look at the rest of the property. Old snow crunched lightly under their boots as they walked across the pasture behind the barn.

"Are those the trees where your grandparents have seen shapes lurking?" Frank asked, pointing to the forest north of the pasture.

"Yeah," Chet said, "and in that stand of pines to the east." He pointed to the right.

"Coyotes?" Joe suggested.

"Our grandparents didn't think so," Iola said. "They used to see coyotes out here in the old days, but not recently."

"Development keeps pushing the wild animals farther west," Chet noted. "There's talk of putting a mall or an industrial park out here."

"Just what the world needs," Joe said sarcastically, "more urban sprawl."

Chet shrugged. "You can't fight progress."

"You said the Zuis farm is to the north beyond the power lines," Frank said. "And Kendall Ridge Road is at the property's west edge. What's east beyond those pines?"

"A big sloped hill that leads down to an old factory," Chet replied.

"Is the factory still working?" Joe asked.

"They have one or two small businesses out there,

I think," Iola said. "It's kind of a failing enterprise."

"That hill next to it is great for sledding," Chet added, "but it's so steep, you almost need a chairlift to get back up."

As he and the others walked back toward the house, Chet pointed out the numerous small ponds dotting the pastures to the east, as well as some old stone walls and copses of trees. "The farm was a great place to play when we were younger," he concluded. "Lots of hiding places, for hide-and-seek."

"Plenty of places to lurk around, too—if you're intent on causing trouble," Frank noted. "Let's sit down inside and figure out where to start checking for clues."

The others nodded their agreement, and they all walked around the barn toward the rear of the house.

As they passed the barn doors, a loud roar sounded from inside. Without warning, both doors burst open and a huge tractor barreled out, heading straight toward them.

2 Death on Wheels

"Look out!" Joe called. He grabbed Iola and dove out of the way.

Chet and Frank jumped aside as the tractor lurched toward them. Chet landed face-first in a small snow bank. Frank turned his leap into a roll and landed on his feet.

"Are you all right?" Joe asked Iola as he got up. Iola nodded. She looked frightened but unhurt.

Frank ran toward the tractor with Joe right behind. No one was steering, and its big engine revved loudly as it rumbled toward the house. The teens followed quickly. Bernie the dog sprinted after them, barking and running circles around the tractor.

Chet spat the snow from his mouth and called,

"Don't hurt the tractor! Our grandparents need it!"

Joe smiled grimly as he ran. "Maybe he should be telling the tractor not to hurt us!" The Hardys easily caught up with the runaway machine; it wasn't moving very quickly. Frank said, "Give me a boost into the seat."

Joe clenched his fingers together in a makeshift step, and Frank put his left foot into Joe's hands. The younger Hardy heaved, vaulting his brother toward the saddle of the tractor.

Frank caught the back of the seat and swung himself up to the controls. He reached the steering wheel and twisted it left just in time to avoid plowing into Bernie's doghouse. The tractor lurched across the snow-crusted driveway and out toward the eastern pastures. The Morton's sheepdog jumped out of the way of the lumbering juggernaut just in time.

Joe had fallen behind after giving Frank a boost, but caught up quickly as the runaway machine turned.

"There's no key to turn it off!" Frank called. He pulled the choke out, and the engine slowed a bit. He tried the control pedals, but nothing happened. "Both the gas and brake are stuck!"

"Help me up and I'll pull the distributor plugs," Joe shouted back. The tractor was an older machine with an open-sided engine case, which made some of its wiring accessible.

Frank extended one hand to Joe while continuing to drive with the other. Joe swung up beside his brother, then reached forward toward the tractor's nose. But the younger Hardy's thick gloves made it difficult to seize the correct cables. After fumbling twice, Joe finally grabbed hold and pulled the wires from the distributor cap with a firm jerk.

With that, the runaway tractor sputtered to a halt. Frank and Joe sighed with relief. "Another minute, and I'd have figured out how to work the clutch on this thing," Frank said apologetically.

"Another minute, and you'd have been in that pond there," Joe said, pointing to a nearby snow-encrusted waterhole.

Frank nodded. "Thanks for pulling the plug," he said. "These old machines are trickier to operate than modern ones."

He and Joe lowered themselves to the ground, and Bernie came over and ran excitedly around their feet.

As the brothers caught their breath, Chet, Iola, and a man the Hardys didn't recognize came running from the barn toward them. The stranger was tall and lean, with a thin face and balding head. He was dressed in grease-stained overalls, a plaid flannel shirt, and scuffed black boots.

"I am *so* sorry," the man blurted as he and the Mortons caught up to the brothers. "I was working on the tractor and it just got away from me." He puffed out white clouds of breath into the snow-dappled air.

"This is Bill Backstrom," Chet explained. "He's one of our local farmhands. He lives just up the road."

"Just about the *only* local hand," Backstrom said. "A lot of the hired help don't like these cold, Bayport winters. I do most of the farm's mechanical work. Thanks for keepin' this from becomin' a real mess."

Joe and Frank shook hands with him. "No problem," Joe said. "We never shy away from a little excitement."

"What in the world is going on out here?" shouted Grandpa Morton's voice. He came dashing out of the farmhouse's back door with Grandma right behind. They both looked worried and angry.

"We had a bit of an accident," Backstrom replied. "I was workin' on ol' Bess when she up an' leaped out the barn door."

Both Grandma and Grandpa Morton crossed their arms over their chests and raised their eyebrows at him.

Backstrom turned red. "Don't ask me to explain it, 'cause I can't," he said. "A lot of strange things have been goin' on around here recently."

"What do you think might have happened?" Grandpa Morton asked.

"Well, nothin' I was doing should have caused the tractor to barrel off that way," Backstrom replied. "It could be that someone got into the barn and messed with the machine somehow—jammed the throttle open or something."

"They jammed the brake, too," Frank added.

"Or maybe it just got iced up," Grandpa replied. "That seems a more reasonable explanation. There's plenty of snow and ice around here nowadays." Bernie barked loudly, as though agreeing with his master.

"Could be, I suppose," Backstrom said. "That part of the barn ain't too well heated. I better take ol' Bess back inside and get her fixed. Better fetch my coat first, though." He hurried back into the barn to retrieve his jacket.

"Sometimes I think that man would forget his own head if it weren't attached," Grandma Morton said. The others chuckled.

"No harm done, I guess," Grandpa replied. "I'm glad you boys managed to get the tractor stopped before it hurt anyone or broke anything up."

"Let's get back in the house before we all freeze," Grandma said.

"What about the tractor?" Joe asked.

"I figure if it got away from Bill and ran out here, he can run it back in," Grandma Morton replied.

As they all turned to go inside, a blue, late-model sedan rumbled up the driveway.

Grandpa Morton frowned. "Well, it figures she'd show up," he said.

"Who?" the four teens asked simultaneously.

"Gail Sanchez," Grandma replied, mirroring her husband's frown, "the lady from the farm supply company." She sighed. "She's seen us, so I suppose we can't pretend we're not home."

"Why would you pretend not to be home?" Frank asked.

"Well, she wants us to switch to her company," Mr. Morton explained, "and she's a bit pushy."

"More than a bit," Grandma added.

The car stopped near the group, and a fashionable brunette in a fur-trimmed coat got out. She took off her dark glasses and smiled at the Mortons.

"Well, what do we have here?" she asked. "A family reunion?"

"Close enough, Ms. Sanchez," Grandpa Morton replied. "What can we do for you today?"

Ms. Sanchez flashed a perfect smile. "It's not what you can do for me, Dave," she said. "It's what *I* can do for *you*." She looked around the property appraisingly and quickly spotted Backstrom, who had returned from the barn and was working on the tractor. "I could set you up with a new tractor, for one thing."

"We like our old tractor, thank you," Grandpa replied.

"But it's practically a *dinosaur*," Ms. Sanchez said. "Really, I could get you very affordable payments on a much nicer one."

"Ms. Sanchez," Grandma Morton said, "we've been with our farm co-op for thirty years—"

"Then it's high time you had an upgrade to something more modern," Ms. Sanchez said. "You'd be amazed what my company can do for you. You can even order supplies over the Internet."

"And have 'em delivered by a computer?" Grandpa retorted wryly.

Ms. Sanchez looked momentarily flustered. "Well, of course not," she finally replied. "But it would be a lot more convenient than driving into town. Tell you what. I'll drop by with some more information in the next day or two."

"You're welcome to visit," Grandpa said, "but we still ain't interested."

"Oh, I'm sure you will be," Ms. Sanchez said confidently. "See you soon." She climbed into her new car and headed back down the driveway to the road.

"'Pushy' is the word I'd use to describe that woman," Joe said.

The Hardys and the Mortons went back inside and warmed up for a while. Grandma Morton fed them hot chocolate and more cookies as they sat by the fire and chatted. Despite some careful prodding by the Hardys, the Morton grandparents avoided mentioning any difficulties with the farm.

After their snack, the four teens did some household chores before dinner. They heard the tractor start up while they were working, and went to the window in time to see Bill Backstrom drive Bess slowly back into the barn. Bernie ran rings around the tractor, barking playfully as the machine rolled along.

Dusk came early to Bayport during the wintertime. Upon finishing their chores, the teens set the table and the Morton grandparents served a hearty farm dinner: chicken and dumplings with carrots and peas, and apple cider. A third course of cookies for dessert left everyone feeling very well fed.

After washing the dishes, they all retired to the Mortons' living room and played games in front of the fireplace. Grandpa Morton quickly got a nice blaze going. Both Frank and Joe challenged Grandpa to chess, but neither brother managed to win. Grandma trounced Chet and Iola at Chinese checkers.

All four teens headed for bed shortly after nine P.M. The Hardys retired to their guest bunks on the second floor while Chet and Iola went to their usual rooms.

"I'm worn out," Joe said, stifling a yawn.

"And we didn't even do much regular farm work today," Frank commented. "Tomorrow will probably be even tougher."

"I think stopping a runaway tractor, helping to clean the house, and doing the dishes is enough for our first day here," Joe replied.

Frank yawned. "I guess so."

In less than twenty minutes, both brothers were sound asleep. But soon they woke with a start. At first, neither Hardy realized what had woken them up. The clock near their bunk read five past midnight. It was pitch black, inside and out.

Suddenly a piercing scream broke the silence.

Joe dropped quickly from his upper bunk to the floor. "That was Iola!"

3 Shadows in the Darkness

Frank leaped down beside Joe.

"Come on!" the younger Hardy said. Despite being barefoot and in their pajamas, both brothers dashed out the bedroom door. They flew down the stairs to the first floor, and skidded to a halt outside Iola's door. Chet, wrapping a bathrobe around his body, arrived just behind.

"Iola, are you all right?" Joe called, knocking on the door. Grandma and Grandpa Morton, both in nightshirts, quickly appeared beside Joe.

Iola's door swung open and she appeared in the doorway, clutching a robe around herself. She looked frightened.

"What's the matter?" Frank asked.

"I . . . I saw someone lurking outside," Iola

23

blurted. She pointed toward a window overlooking the backyard and barn.

Joe immediately crossed to the window and gazed out. Grandma Morton had come with a flashlight, and she promptly handed it to Joe. They turned off the lights so they could see outside. "I don't see anyone," he said, pointing the flashlight beam on the snow. Peering at the ground outside, he added, "No sign of any footprints, either." He turned the lights in the room on again.

"He wasn't right outside my window," Iola said. "He was sneaking around between the house and the barn."

"Bill Backstrom, maybe?" Frank suggested.

"Bill should be home and in bed by now," Grandma replied.

"Well, if it was anybody else, Bernie would be barking his head off," Grandpa Morton said. "He's a good watchdog."

"Maybe you imagined it?" Chet said. "With the snow blowing around, and the shadows from the nearby trees . . ."

"Chet Morton," Iola shot back angrily, "I am *not* imagining things! I definitely saw someone skulking around the backyard."

"Well, there's no one there now, sweetheart," Grandma Morton said sympathetically.

"Let's check it out," Joe suggested to Frank. Both Hardys headed for the back door. They swiftly donned their boots and coats in the mudroom, took the flashlight, and hurried outside.

Blowing snowflakes danced on the night wind, though no new snow was actually falling at the moment. Frank and Joe took a bearing from Iola's window, and then traced her line of sight across the driveway and over toward the barn.

"This is no good," Joe said, frustrated. "With all the traffic on the driveway today, there's no way we'll find any decent prints here."

"Not in this light, anyway," Frank agreed. "This flashlight is pretty weak. Maybe tomorrow morning we can turn something up."

"Yeah, maybe," Joe replied, but he sounded doubtful.

The four Mortons, all with coats bundled over their nightclothes, met the brothers outside as the Hardys returned to the house.

"Find anything?" Iola asked hopefully.

"It's too dark," Frank replied.

"And too cold to be prowling around even if there were anything to see," Grandma Morton cautioned.

"We'll check tomorrow, when the light's better," Joe said. He put a sturdy arm around Iola's shoulder.

"What about you, you old dust mop!" Grandpa Morton bellowed irritably to the nearby doghouse. He bent down and peered into the front opening, looking for Bernie.

Inside, the old sheepdog slept soundly.

"Well, I'll be . . . ," Grandpa said. "Imagine this bag of fur sleeping through all this commotion!" He reached down and pulled on Bernie's collar.

Bernie lazily opened his eyes and peered out from beneath his gray and white bangs.

"Some watchdog!" Grandpa scolded. "Come on! Get up and earn your keep."

Reluctantly, the dog stood and shook himself. He blinked sleepily and gazed around the group.

"Don't be so hard on him, Grandpa," Iola said. "He looks tired."

"Well, now *all* of us are tired, 'cause 'man's best friend' here's been sleeping on the job," Grandpa replied.

Grandma tried not to snicker. "I'll get him some fresh water," she said. "His bowl is frozen over."

"Maybe you better make it coffee," Chet quipped.

They all laughed. Grandma freshened Bernie's water, then all the Mortons went back inside and returned to bed. Joe and Frank sat up awhile and kept watch outside the kitchen window.

Spotting nothing unusual, they finally gave up and returned to bed as well. The last thing they saw before creeping back upstairs was Bernie, sitting in the snow outside his doghouse, gazing patiently into the night.

* * * *

Dawn came early on the Morton farm. Winter was a slow season for them, but there were still plenty of chores to be done.

The family ate a hearty breakfast of pancakes, bacon, and eggs. No one mentioned the incident from last night, but Joe and Frank could tell that the intruder wasn't far from anyone's mind.

After breakfast the Hardys and their friends set to their chores. The brothers volunteered to help Chet and Iola take care of the animals. On their way to the barn, the four teens passed Bernie, who seemed too tired to play.

They found Bill Backstrom inside, still working on the malfunctioning tractor.

"Hey, Bill," Chet said as they headed toward the back of the barn, "were you working here late last night?"

"How late?" Backstrom asked.

"Around midnight," Frank replied.

"Nope," Backstrom said. "I headed home around nine. That was plenty late enough for me. Say, which wires did you mess with when you stopped the tractor yesterday?"

"Just the distributor wires," Joe said.

Backstrom shook his head. "Well, somehow the starter got crosswired. Maybe that's why ol' Bess went haywire yesterday."

"Could a small animal have stripped the starter wires, causing the short circuit?" Frank asked.

27

"Not likely," Bill replied. "'Course, sometimes animals do crawl into the machinery—especially when it's cold and the engine is warm. But I've yet to meet a varmint who could hotwire a tractor." He sighed and rubbed his balding head. "I'll figure it out eventually."

"Good luck," Joe said as he and the others headed toward the pens in the barn's addition.

As they walked, Chet whispered, "Iola and I can handle these chores, if you guys want to do some investigating."

Frank shook his head. "It's still not light enough to get a good look around."

"Besides," Joe added, "what would your grandparents say if we left you to do the chores alone? They'd probably put us in the doghouse with Bernie."

"No they wouldn't," Iola replied. "They knew this would be vacation time for you. They wouldn't compare you to that lazy old dog."

"Bernie isn't really that old," Chet said. "He's only six. I'm surprised he fell asleep like that."

"Maybe he wore himself out chasing the tractor," Joe suggested.

"I guess," Chet replied. "But Grandpa was right when he said Bernie's usually a good watchdog."

"Even if he is," Frank said, "we'd better keep our own eyes peeled—just in case."

The brothers and their friends milked the cows, groomed the horses, and then cleaned the stalls.

By the time they'd finished, the morning sun was creeping toward high noon. The air had grown warmer, too, melting off some of the snowfall.

"If we're going to look for tracks," Joe said, "we better do it before they all melt away."

All four of them circled around the barn, checking for anything out of the ordinary. Their own footprints and those of Bill, the Morton grandparents, and Bernie made quite a confusing mess. Finally they discovered two sets of tracks leading away from the back of the barn toward the woods on the north side of the property.

"It looks like that's the way the intruder came," Frank said.

"And left," Joe added. "One set of prints in each direction. I don't think these were here when you gave us the tour yesterday."

Iola nodded. "So either someone dropped by while we were working . . ."

"Or, I'd say we've found your phantom, Iola," Frank said, finishing her thought.

Frank stooped down and picked something out of one of the impressions in the snow. It was a small metal circlet about an inch wide.

"What's that?" Joe asked.

"It looks like it might be part of a horse's tack," Iola said.

Chet shook his head. "It's not big enough, or stout enough."

Frank thought for a moment, turning the ring over in his hand. "I think it's a grommet from a chin strap."

"Like a from a motorcycle helmet," Joe said.

"Or motorcycle boot strap," Frank agreed. "Whoever made these tracks must have lost it." He tucked the ring into one of his jacket pockets.

"Let's see where the tracks lead," Joe suggested.

"Can we grab some lunch first?" Chet asked. "After this morning's chores, I'm starving."

"Chet's right," Frank said. "And tracking through the snow and rough terrain will be tough. We'll need all the energy we can get. Since whoever made those footprints is long gone, we might as well stoke up first."

The others agreed, and they all returned to the house. Frank made toasted bologna and cheese sandwiches for everyone, while Chet made hot cocoa. Joe and Iola set the table and called the Morton grandparents to eat, then ferried food out to Bill Backstrom. The teens brought Bernie inside and fed him, as well.

Just as they were all finishing lunch, someone knocked on the back door. Bernie immediately began barking loudly.

"Hello!" called a friendly voice. "Anyone at home?"

"Come on in," Grandpa said, taking hold of the dog's collar. In swept a woman dressed in a maroon business dress and fashionable coat. With her came two gray-suited men carrying briefcases.

"Hello," the woman said, "I'm Patsy Stein. I talked to you on the phone a couple of days ago."

Grandma and Grandpa Morton nodded. "We remember," Grandpa said.

Ms. Stein smiled curtly. "I just wanted to stop by in person and drop off some papers, so you can see that my offer is genuine."

"What offer?" Chet asked suspiciously.

Ms. Stein smiled indulgently at him. "Well, I think that's for Marge and Dave to announce, not me," she replied.

"She wants to buy the farm," Grandpa explained.

Iola and Chet both looked shocked. "Are you going to sell it?" Iola asked.

Before either of her grandparents could answer, Patsy Stein broke in. "They're still making up their minds," she said. "But I'm sure that after they look over the details of my plan, we'll be able to reach some agreement."

"She wants to put up a mall," Grandma explained.

"Not just any mall," Ms. Stein said, "a *premier* mall, designed with the sensibilities of the current shopper in mind."

"But doesn't Bayport have enough malls?" Joe asked rhetorically. "It's not malls we're running out of, it's farms and open spaces."

Ms. Stein grinned at him and asked, "Are you one of the Morton grandchildren?" Turning to the

31

Mortons, she added, "You must be so proud."

"Actually, he's a guest," Grandpa replied, starting to look steamed. "And we already told you over the phone, we're just not interested."

Ms. Stein ignored his refusal. "If you'll just look at our offer," she said. One of the men accompanying her stepped forward and opened his briefcase. He laid some papers out on the kitchen table.

"I don't mean to be rude," Grandma Morton said, rising from her seat, "but you're interrupting our lunch. Leave your information if you like. We'll get in touch with you if we have any interest."

"Thanks. That's all I'm asking," Ms. Stein said. Her associate shut his briefcase, and all three of them left.

"Pushy must be the thing to be this year," Iola commented after they'd gone.

"And why'd she bring two extra guys with her?" Chet added.

"Intimidation, maybe," Frank suggested.

"Probably, knowing that Stein woman," Grandpa said grumpily. "She just won't take no for an answer."

"She and Gail Sanchez should get together," Joe said. "They could form a club: Stubborn Salespeople Anonymous."

"Well, you kids needn't worry about either of them," Grandma said. "Go outside and have some fun. Grandpa and I will clear the dishes."

"Are you sure?" Iola asked.

"You've done enough making lunch," Grandpa said. "Enjoy yourselves awhile. We don't want your friends' vacation to be *all* work."

"Thanks, Grandma and Grandpa," Chet said. The four friends put on their coats and went back around the barn to the tracks they'd discovered earlier.

"We could ride after them," Iola suggested. "The horses could use some exercise anyway."

"Good idea," Joe agreed.

They went into the stables behind the barn and saddled up all four of the Mortons' horses. The horses seemed eager to run after being cooped up due to bad weather. They plodded happily through the snow, toward the forest on the north side of the property.

"Who did you say owns the property beyond those woods?" Joe asked.

"J. J. Zuis owns the house up on the hill," Chet replied, "but the Costellos own the plot to the northeast."

"Those are the unfriendly neighbors, right?" Frank asked.

"Right," Iola replied.

"And of course the power company has right-of-way around the high-tension lines," Chet finished. "They've got a service road there, too."

"I doubt last night's intruder was an electric company employee who'd come to read the meter," Joe joked.

The horses knew the Morton land better than any of the teens. They crossed the snowy fields quickly, deftly avoiding the numerous ruts and half-buried farm ponds. The snow melted away at the treeline, though, and the tracks petered out a short distance into the woods. The four teens tethered their horses and walked into the forest, crouching close to the ground and looking for signs of the intruder.

"Rats!" Joe said as the ground became progressively more bare. "Looks like we should have come out earlier after all."

"It might not have done any good anyway," Frank said. "The pine tree canopy has kept most of the snow off the ground here. Even this morning we probably wouldn't have found anything."

"So what's next?" Chet asked hopefully.

"Next, we—," Joe began, but a sudden noise stopped him in mid-sentence.

CRACK!

"Get down!" Frank cried. "Someone's shooting at us!"

4 Winter Hunt

All four teens dived to the ground, looking for cover. But the needle-covered forest floor was clear of brush, and the tree trunks weren't big enough to hide behind.

CRACK!

Another shot, closer this time.

"Sounds like a rifle," Frank said.

"Can you see the gunman?" Joe asked. "Where are the bullets coming from?" He swung his head around, looking in all directions.

"I don't know," Frank replied. His keen brown eyes scanned the woods nearby but found nothing. "He must be behind one of the larger trees."

"Are you sure he's shooting at *us*?" Iola said. "Maybe it's just a hunter."

"Well, I think teenagers are out of season," Chet quipped.

CRACK!

"C'mon," Frank said. He sprang up and ran northwest, farther into the forest. The others dashed after him.

"Should we be leaving the horses?" Chet asked.

"The horses are big targets, plus they're tied up out in the open," Joe replied. "The sniper could have killed them already if he wanted to. They'll be fine." The younger Hardy held tight to Iola's hand as he ran, making sure she didn't fall behind.

They sprinted through the soggy winter woods, their boots crunching on pine needles and small patches of snow.

CRACK!

"Are you sure we're going the right way?" Iola asked.

"Not entirely," Frank replied. "We should split up, instead of giving him one big target."

"Chet, you and Iola keep going straight," Joe said. "Frank and I will circle around to the northeast."

"But I think the shots are coming from there," Chet said.

Frank nodded. "Hopefully—that'll give you both a chance to circle back to the horses and go for help," he said.

"Joe, no!" Iola pleaded. Tears formed at the corners of her gray eyes.

"It's the only way," Joe replied. "Don't worry. Frank and I can take care of ourselves."

"With luck," Frank added, "we may be able to 'take care' of this sniper, too." He locked eyes with his friends. "We split on three. Ready? One, two . . . three!"

Frank and Joe veered off to the right while Chet and Iola kept running northwest.

CRACK!

A bullet whizzed through the pine branches somewhere behind the Hardys. It didn't come anywhere near the Mortons.

"I think our ploy worked," Joe said as they ran.

"Good," Frank replied. "Keep your eyes peeled for that sniper. The trees are getting thicker ahead. We'll be able to find some cover and catch our breath."

The brothers darted into a thick stand of pines and took refuge behind a boulder. The rock was only shoulder height, but it was wide enough to shield both of them from the rifleman. A small drift of partially melted snow clung to the north side of the rock.

"We don't want him cutting around behind us," Joe cautioned.

"We should be able to hear him coming if he tries," Frank said.

Both brothers held their breath and listened. To the north, the woods thinned out. They caught glimpses of white snow beyond.

"That must be the right-of-way for the power lines," Joe whispered.

Frank nodded.

"Do you hear something?" Joe asked.

Frank nodded slowly. "It's coming from near the right-of-way."

"He's circling us," Joe hissed, "trying to cut us off."

"Let's beat him to the punch," Frank said. He scooped up a double handful of the slushy ice and formed it into a hard-packed snowball. Joe grabbed a big stick from the ground nearby.

They paused a moment, trying to further pinpoint the source of the noise. As they watched, a slender figure darted between the trees, heading toward the open area beneath the power lines.

"He's lost track of us!" Frank whispered. "Now's our chance!"

Both teens sprinted out from behind the boulder toward the fleeting shape. The pine needles blanketing the forest floor made for almost ideal running conditions. It was no trouble to leap the few fallen branches and small snowdrifts barring their way.

The brothers covered the fifty yards separating them from their quarry in seconds.

Hearing them, the figure turned at the last instant.

Frank launched his snowball, using all the skill

he'd learned as a pitcher for the Bayport High baseball team. The icy mass caught the intruder square on the side of the head. He went down at the edge of the right-of-way, crashing to the snow-covered earth with a muffled grunt.

Before he could rise again, both Frank and Joe cornered him.

"You'll stay down if you know what's good for you!" Joe said, brandishing his stick like a club.

The intruder cowered at the Hardys feet, keeping one arm near his head to protect himself in case Joe hit him. The brothers' foe was a tall teenager with scruffy black hair and a narrow face. A navy blue down jacket, snow pants, and winter boots covered his slender frame.

"Are you guys crazy?" the teen asked angrily. "What do you think you're doing?"

"We'd like to ask you the same thing," Frank replied. "Why were you taking pot shots at us?"

"Pot shots?" the teen said. "What are you talking about? I don't have a gun." He showed the brothers his empty hands. "I thought *you* guys were the ones shooting."

Joe's blue eyes scanned the snow-dappled clearing. "I don't see any gun, Frank," he said.

"Who are you?" the intruder demanded angrily.

We're Frank and Joe Hardy," Frank replied. "We're staying with the Mortons."

"The Mortons!" the teen said. "That explains it."

"What do you mean?" Joe asked.

"The Mortons have been making trouble for my family for generations," the teen replied. "I'm Elan Costello."

"What are you doing on the Mortons' property?" Frank asked.

"For your information," Costello replied, "we're not *on* the Mortons' property. *You're* on *our* property. This is the Costello farm, you jerks. The Morton property ends at the edge of that forest."

"Says you!" came a cry from nearby.

Chet and Iola rode out of the woods toward the Hardys, with Frank and Joe's horses in tow. Both Chet and Iola glared at Elan Costello.

"Our property may end at the woods," Chet continued, "but *his* property doesn't start until the other side of the right-of-way."

"So, technically, this is no man's land," Iola said.

"You're wrong, Morton," Costello replied, rising to his feet. "Our property line cuts through the edge of the woods here, and continues on the other side of the lines. You all are trespassing in *my* land."

"Don't listen to him," Chet said to Frank and Joe. "He's a well-known troublemaker."

Costello sneered at him. "Big talk from a big man, Morton," he said. "Why don't you get off your high horse and say that to my face."

"Maybe I will," Chet replied, slipping from the

saddle. Before he could cross the distance separating the them, though, a sound like thunder shook the air.

BLAM!

All five teenagers turned and saw another man, dressed in a blue parka and tall white cowboy hat, striding across from them. In his suede-gloved hands the man carried a pump-action shotgun. The muzzle of the gun smoked slightly.

"Hold it right there, Morton," the man said. "Don't take another step toward my boy."

"That's Elan's dad: Vic," Iola whispered.

"He was taking shots at us as we rode through the woods!" Chet said angrily.

"Well," Mr. Costello replied dryly, "seems to me that if you were *trespassing*, he had a right to shoot at you. You got your gun with you, Elan?"

"No, Pa," Elan replied.

"Lucky thing I do, then," Vic said. "You never know what kind of varmints you might run into on the back forty."

"This isn't your land," Iola said nervously. "It belongs to the power company."

Vic Costello spat into the snow. "A technicality," he said. "It was Costello land before they put up these metal monsters, and it'll be Costello land again once the towers have rusted away."

"That could take a while," Joe noted. "You might not want to wait around."

The elder Costello's gray eyes narrowed. "I see

the Mortons' guests are as short on manners as the Mortons themselves," he said. He spat again.

Elan Costello brushed the snow off his coat. "Go on home, all of you," he said, "before we call the cops."

"Call 'em if you want—," Joe began, but Frank put his hand on his brother's shoulder, stopping him in mid-rebuff.

"We'll leave," the elder Hardy replied. "But we'll be keeping an eye out for more intruders on the Morton land. If we see any, then *we'll* be the ones calling the police."

The Costellos didn't reply. They merely glared at the four friends.

"Come on," Chet finally said. "Let's get back to the house."

All four teens saddled up and rode back into the woods, being careful to skirt around the edge of the Costello property.

"No sense giving them another chance to shoot at us," Chet said angrily.

"Actually," Frank said, "I'm not sure they *did* shoot at us. Mr. Costello had a shotgun, not a rifle."

"And it was a rifle shooting at us in the woods," Joe continued. "We could tell from the sound."

"But if Elan and his father weren't shooting at us," Iola said, "who was?"

Frank and Joe both shook their heads.

"It might be the same person who was lurking

outside the house last night," Joe said. "But right now, we just don't have enough clues to form a good hypothesis."

All four of them rode back to the Morton farm in silence. The sky clouded over and a steady snow began to fall. It was nearly a blizzard by the time they got back to the house.

They put the horses up in the barn, then rubbed the animals down and groomed them. Then the four friends hiked back through the barn toward the big white farmhouse. The snow was falling even more heavily now, and a blustery wind had already begun piling up small drifts all around.

As the teens crossed the driveway, Grandma and Grandpa Morton pulled up in the family station wagon. Huge bags of groceries filled the back of the car. The brothers and their friends carried the food in, then helped to put it away.

"I know your brother eats a lot," Joe said to Iola as he stuffed another can of tuna into the pantry, "but this much grub could feed a whole army of Chets!"

Chet laughed and slugged Joe in the arm.

"We're stocking up," Grandpa explained. "The weatherman says we're going to get a heap of snow over the next few days. We need to make sure we have plenty of provisions in case we get snowed in."

"Do you think that's likely?" Frank asked.

Grandma Morton shrugged. "It's happened before,"

she said, "and it'll happen again. If not this winter, then the next, or the one after that."

"It's been a while since Bayport's last big blizzard," Grandpa noted. "We're due for another." He finished stocking some bottles of lantern kerosene under a cupboard near the sink.

"That'd make an interesting twist to our vacation," Joe said.

"It wouldn't be so bad," Iola insisted. "We have plenty of candles and lanterns, and all three fireplaces work really well. This old farmhouse can stay pretty toasty, even without modern power and heat."

"Don't go counting on a snow day yet," Grandma replied, laughing. "If this blizzard hits—like the weathermen think it will—we'll deal with it. Until then, there's still plenty to do around here."

"We'll haul the lamps out and get the extra blankets ready, just in case," Grandpa said. "Come on. You youngsters can help. The barn needs readying too."

They finished putting away the supplies, then went back to the stables and made sure the animals were prepared for the coming storm. The clouds were creeping toward dark when everyone finally headed back inside.

"What about Bernie?" Joe asked. "Will he be okay in his doghouse?"

"We'll take him inside with us for the night, just

in case," Grandpa said. He gazed up at the iron gray sky. Thick, white flakes tumbled down. He caught one on his tongue and smacked his lips.

The teens all laughed and did the same.

As they did, Grandpa Morton went to the doghouse to fetch Bernie. "Come on, boy!" he called. "You get to spend tonight inside with the rest of the family."

He pulled on the dog chain lying in front of the small shelter, but it came out of the house empty.

Grandpa frowned. "Now, how could that dog have gotten himself loose?" he asked. He leaned down to the doghouse door and called, "Bernie, where are you, you rag mop?"

When Bernie still didn't come out, he reached inside and fished around for the dog's collar. A moment later he pulled out his hand again. In it he held a small piece of white paper. He looked perplexed.

"What's that?" Iola asked.

"It looks like a note," Joe said.

Grandpa Morton didn't reply, but held out the paper so they could read the plain, block letters written on it.

The message read, IF YOU WANT TO DO WHAT'S BEST FOR YOUR DOG, PACK IT IN NOW, BEFORE THERE'S MORE TROUBLE.

5 Dog Gone

Grandpa Morton's eyes narrowed. "Is this some kind of a joke?" he asked the teens. "Did one of you kids hide Bernie in the barn while I wasn't looking?"

Chet shook his head. "Not us, Grandpa."

"When was the last time anyone saw him?" Frank asked.

"I tied him up in the doghouse before we left for the store," Grandpa Morton said.

"I didn't notice him when you got back," Iola said.

"I just assumed he was taking a nap in his doghouse," Grandpa said. "He was up most of last night, so I didn't think anything of it."

"We didn't either," Joe said. "That means he could have been stolen any time during the afternoon—

either while we were out riding in the woods, or when we were grooming the horses, or even while we were putting the groceries away."

"You'd have to be a pretty bold dognapper to take him while all of us were in the house," Frank noted. "We could have heard something if we'd been around."

"Bernie might be friendly," Iola said, "but he wouldn't let a stranger take him away without putting up a fight."

Frank nodded. "That's why I think it's more likely the dognapping happened before Grandpa and Grandma Morton came home."

"In that amount of time," Chet said, "Elan Costello could have sneaked back onto our property and done it himself."

"It wouldn't surprise me after the trouble we had with him and his father in the woods," Iola added.

"What trouble was that?" Mr. Morton asked.

The teens explained about the gunshots in the woods and their confrontation with the Costellos.

"Why didn't you mention this earlier?" Grandpa asked, going a little red in the face.

"We didn't want to worry you," Iola replied.

"And I certainly am worried," Grandpa said, shaking his head. "Kidnapping a dog seems low, even for Costello, but shooting is worse," he added. "We better call the police."

Before the police were called, the Hardys checked

around for clues about the dog's whereabouts, but their trudging around the doghouse had wiped out any tracks they might have found.

The Mortons called Bill Backstrom, who had gone home early in anticipation of the storm, and he hadn't seen Bernie all afternoon. They called some of the other neighbors, including J. J. Zuis and the Costellos, to make sure Bernie hadn't just wandered off. None of the neighbors had seen the big sheep-dog. The Mortons finally decided to call the police.

An hour and a half later a Bayport PD patrol car pulled up the long driveway of the Morton farm. Two officers, a young woman and an older man, walked up the drift-covered path to the front door. The Morton grandparents let them inside and invited them into the kitchen for coffee.

The Hardys had met one of the cops before. He was an old, gruff patrolman named Gus Sullivan. The young blond officer wore a name tag that read JULIE SCOTT. Sullivan and Scott seated themselves at the kitchen table and listened to the Mortons' story while sipping coffee.

"The roads are in bad shape," Officer Sullivan explained. "We've been taking car-wreck calls most of the afternoon. A truck jackknifed into a tele-phone pole out on Highway Eleven."

Frank and Joe glanced warily at each other. Clearly Sullivan didn't seem happy to have come all this way for a missing dog.

"You're sure the dog didn't just wander off?" Officer Scott asked.

"Look at this note," Grandma said, handing them the paper they'd found in the doghouse.

The police examined the note, glanced at each other, and nodded. "Do you know this note wasn't there before?" Officer Sullivan asked. "It could have been left by one of those animal rights people. They don't like to see dogs chained up outside when it's cold. Some people think they know how to handle farm animals better than the farmers themselves."

"There have been notes like that left in rural Bayport before," Officer Scott agreed, "just to warn dog owners about what these activists perceive as a problem."

"You'll let us know if there's a ransom demand," Sullivan said.

"You don't think this counts as a threat?" Chet asked, incredulous.

Officer Scott shrugged. "It could just be a stunt. Farm kids have strange senses of humor, sometimes. But neither an activist nor a kid would want to keep the dog. I expect he'll be back in the next day or two, if he doesn't wander back on his own sooner. These pranks never last very long."

"If it is a prank, it's not very funny," Iola commented.

"Now look here, Officers," Grandma said. "I know this may not be much to police officers like you, but Bernie is part of our family. He's also a purebred English sheepdog—worth quite a bit, even without his papers."

"We don't have any reports of other dogs going missing—purebred or otherwise," Officer Scott replied, "but we'll surely check into it. I've had a few dogs myself and I know what it's like to lose one."

"It may take a while," Sullivan added, "with all the trouble this storm is brewing up."

"We'll appreciate whatever you can do," Grandma said.

The officers thanked them for the coffee and then returned to their patrol car.

"Do you think they'll actually *do* anything?" Chet asked the Hardys as the police car drove away.

"Hard to say," Frank replied. "This storm may keep them pretty busy."

"Even with the storm," Iola said, "I don't feel right just sitting here while Bernie's missing."

"We could take another look around," Joe suggested. "It'll be getting dark soon, but maybe we can turn up something before nightfall."

"It's worth a shot," Frank agreed.

"You just be careful out there," Grandma called from the kitchen. "We don't want any missing children in addition to the missing dog."

The brothers and the Morton teens bundled up again and headed out into the storm. They grabbed some flashlights, in case their exploration took longer than they expected. A north wind howled around the farm, blowing dancing clouds of flakes into the air and whistling through the cracks in the old barn.

"We'll circle around the house and barn," Frank said, "and see if we spot anything unusual."

The others nodded, and all four of them trudged around the house, looking for signs of Bernie or anything unusual. In the pasture on the west side of the barn, not too far from the driveway, they found a long, straight track in the snow.

"Snowmobile?" Joe asked.

Frank nodded.

"I don't remember anyone visiting on a snow-mobile today," Chet said.

"And I don't remember hearing one, either," Iola added.

"We might not hear them in this wind," Joe commented, "but the tracks don't look very fresh. See how the drifting snow has already filled in the tread marks?"

"Whoever rode through here must have come while we were in the woods and the Mortons were away," Frank deduced.

"That seems a reasonable conclusion," said Joe. "And if that's true, whoever drove this snow-mobile might have something to do with Bernie's disappearance."

Frank snapped his fingers. "Remember that metal

grommet we found earlier? Maybe it was from some *snowmobile* gear—not motorcycle gear."

"That makes sense," Joe said. He and the others gazed at the trail leading away from the barn.

The tracks led through the pastures to the east. The friends couldn't tell how far they went because the snowfall limited their vision.

"Let's follow the tracks," Joe said.

"It'd take a while on foot, and the snow is piling up pretty quick," Frank noted. "Iola, do you think the horses would be up to another ride?"

She shook her head. "Not in this weather," Iola replied. "They're probably still tired from our ride earlier."

Chet smiled. "We don't need horses," he said. "We've got something better."

He led the others to the barn, opened the doors, and pulled the tarp off the old car chassis. "The buggy will let us follow those tracks quicker than we could on horseback."

"Great idea," Frank said, "if you think it's up to running in this snow."

"It'll be a blast," Chet replied. "Though it might get a bit chilly—since the buggy doesn't have any windows, or doors, or a body, or side panels, or . . ."

"It wouldn't be any worse than a snowmobile," Iola countered. "We're dressed for cold weather. Let's do it."

Chet fetched the keys from a peg on the barn wall.

He took the wheel while Frank took the passenger seat beside him. Joe and Iola sat on the bench seat in back, and they all buckled their seat belts.

"Atomic batteries to power; turbines to speed," Chet joked as he turned the key. Almost immediately, the old VW engine behind them sputtered to life.

They pulled out of the barn into the driveway, stopping only long enough to close the barn doors behind them. They went east to the spot where they'd found the snowmobile tracks, then barreled off through the pasture in hot pursuit.

All four teens held on tight as the buggy bounced and jostled over the snowy terrain. Snow blew hard into their faces, and finding exactly where they were going was tricky. Twice Chet barely turned in time to avoid some small farm ponds that appeared suddenly in their way.

"Whoever was on that snowmobile knew the terrain pretty well," Joe said. "They avoided those ponds too."

"Lucky for them," Chet noted. "It hasn't been cold long enough for a really good freeze. The ice on some of the larger ponds might not support a snowmobile yet."

"Or the buggy," Iola noted, "so you better watch where you're going, Chet."

"Will do, commander," Chet replied jovially.

They followed the tracks east, into the tall stand of pines that jutted down from the forest on the north. The trail became less distinct under the trees, but the evergreen branches sheltered the riders from the snow as well, making it easier to see.

"Chances are, the dognapper followed the old road here," Chet said as the tracks petered out under drifting snow. A wide trail kept going east ahead of them. "Cutting through the trees would be pretty dangerous."

"Like a high-speed slalom," Joe said. "A fun ride, but deadly if you make a wrong turn."

"Where does the road go?" Frank asked.

"It splits up ahead," Chet replied. "One branch goes down to the hill by the old factory; the other heads up to the power lines."

"Near the Costello property," Iola added.

When they got to the fork a few minutes later, they stopped to check for signs.

"It looks like snowmobiles have been down *both* of these trails recently," Joe said.

"That makes sense," Iola replied. "This part of the farm is on a registered snowmobile trail. Our grandparents gave the local association permission to use it."

"Snowmobilers usually show up the minute the ground is covered in powder," Chet said. "They don't want to miss a minute of riding after waiting through the summer for the first snowfall."

"Unfortunately," Frank said, "that just makes our job harder. Which way should we go?"

"The factory hill is closer than the power lines," Chet said.

"Let's check it first, then," Joe suggested. "We can always backtrack if we need to."

"Assuming the snow doesn't get any worse," Iola said.

They turned to the right, heading toward the slope on the eastern edge of the Morton property.

The big pine trees flew by, and a few minutes later they broke out of the forest into the open once more. Chet skidded the buggy to a quick halt.

Ahead of them, the ground dropped off in a steep hill. The slope flattened out about thirty yards down and then stretched toward an old factory about a quarter mile away.

"If we take the buggy down there," Chet said, "we'll have to cut over to the main road to get back to the farm. No way we'll make it up the slope again—not in this weather."

"I don't see any snowmobile tracks here," Frank said, pointing to the decline in front of them.

"Let's check along the ridge," Joe suggested.

"We'll have to do it on foot," Iola said. "There's not enough room between the forest and the drop off to maneuver the buggy."

"Plenty of room for a snow mobile, though," Frank noted. "Let's get going. If we don't find anything, we'll take the trail back toward the power lines."

Chet and Iola went south, while Frank and Joe went north. They moved quickly but deliberately through the shin-high snow.

"See anything?" Chet called to the brothers. The two groups were about fifty yards apart now, with the buggy idling in between, near the trail.

"There are definitely some snowmobile tracks this way," Frank called back. "What about you?"

"This way, too," Iola replied. "They're running along the edge of the woods, though, not down the slope."

"The dognapper could have gone either way, then," Joe concluded, "if these are even his tracks at all. Maybe he didn't even go *down* the slope."

"He'd have to," Chet said. "There's no safe way back into the forest. Though they could have followed the ridge line all the way south to the road."

Ahead of the brothers, the trees grew progressively nearer to the slope's edge. A snowmobile couldn't go much farther in that direction.

"Wait a minute!" Frank said, peering through the blowing powder. "It looks like someone cut downslope up ahead."

He and Joe quickly hiked toward the track the elder Hardy had spotted. A small jut of land stuck out right where the slope met the forest. The snowmobile tracks dipped over the edge of the prominence and vanished down the hill.

The brothers stopped at the edge and peered into the snow.

"Do you think we can climb down?" Joe asked.

Frank frowned. "It's getting back up that's probably the problem, but if Chet has some rope in the buggy, it's worth a shot."

Joe turned back the way they'd come and cupped his gloved hands to call to their friends. As he did, the snow beneath his feet gave way.

"Joe!" Frank gasped. He stuck out his hand to grab his brother, but it was too late. Suddenly the snow beneath Frank gave way too, and both Hardys plunged down the precipice.

6 Snowslide

"Joe! Frank!" Iola cried.

She and Chet raced to where the Hardys had disappeared over the edge of the slope, being careful not to fall themselves.

"Frank! Joe! Are you all right?" Chet called.

The Hardys couldn't hear them.

Snow and dirt cascaded all around Frank and Joe. Chilly white powder filled the air, stinging their faces and making it hard to breathe. The Hardys tumbled head over heels, spinning and twisting, unable to resist the avalanche.

"Try to surf it out!" Frank called to his brother. He pumped his arms like a swimmer, attempting to scramble atop the mess.

"Okay, I . . . *ugh!*" Joe yelped as a loose stone struck his calf. The snowslide spun him around, and he disappeared in a cloud of white spray.

"Joe! Joe! Are you—"

Snow smothered Frank's cry. Icy powder rumbled over his face, blinding him and filling his mouth. For a moment he couldn't breathe, couldn't tell up from down. Pieces of ice and rock pelted his body. Fortunately his heavy winter clothes blunted the impact.

He fought to reach the surface of the slide. If he got completely buried, Frank knew his chances of living were slim.

The avalanche slowed. Frank kicked up hard, pushing with his arms. The blizzard of rocks and powder fell away from his face, and he gasped fresh air once more.

"Frank! Frank!" Joe called from nearby.

"I'm all right," Frank sputtered.

Slowly, the snowslide carrying the Hardys ground to a halt.

Frank and Joe found themselves buried up to their shoulders in snow ten yards beyond the bottom of the slope. They could hear Chet and Iola shouting from the top of the bluff, but the wind carried away the Mortons' words.

"Are you okay?" Frank gasped, looking at Joe. He felt bruised and achy, but not badly hurt.

"Yeah, I'm all right."

"We're lucky not to have any broken bones . . . or worse," Frank said.

Joe grunted as he tried to pull himself out of the snow. "I think I'm stuck. What about you?"

The two of them struggled against the snow for a few minutes, but only managed to get their hands and arms free.

"I think we can dig ourselves out," Frank said, "eventually."

"We may freeze first," Joe noted.

Frank twisted his head toward the bluff and cupped his hands to his mouth. "We're okay!" he called up to Chet and Iola. "But we're stuck!"

Chet quickly cupped his hands to his mouth, like Frank had, and called back, "There's a rope in the buggy—I'm going to get it and climb down to you!"

"Be careful!" Joe called back. "Iola, you stay put—we might need to send for help!"

"Check," Iola called. "I'm so glad you're not hurt!"

While Joe and Frank continued trying to work themselves free, Chet fetched the rope from the buggy and tied it to the vehicle's bumper. The big teen slipped a couple of times on his way down, but he finally reached the brothers.

"We're lucky I didn't cause another avalanche," Chet said. He wiped a damp lock of blond hair out of his eyes and began digging with his hands. Unfortunately the slide had compacted the snow, making the digging very difficult. "Remind me to put a shovel in the buggy's trunk when we get home," he said.

Frank and Joe tried to help Chet, but they didn't have much leverage. "We should have brought a cell phone, too," Frank noted.

"Should we send Iola back to the farm for help?" Chet asked.

"Driving through this storm alone would be dangerous," Joe replied. "If something happened to her, it'd be horrible."

"Joe's right. We don't know if the dognappers are still out there," Frank said, "and we don't know what else they're capable of. It's best to stick together as long as we can."

Chet and the Hardys dug for fifteen minutes, but Joe and Frank's lower bodies remained embedded in compacted snow. Ice crystals had formed in the hair of all three boys. They looked like refugees from an Antarctic expedition.

"Hey!" Joe exclaimed. "There's someone walking over there, near the old factory!"

"Hey! Help!" Frank called to the figure. "We're stuck!" The figure paused and peered through the blizzard.

"Give us a hand!" Chet shouted. "We're stuck in the snow!"

For a moment, it seemed the figure might not come to help. Then, slowly, a middle-aged man with graying hair and black plastic glasses trudged toward them out of the snowstorm. "What are you kids doing out here?" he asked suspiciously.

"We got caught in a snowslide," Joe said.

The man's eyes narrowed. "Funny time to be running around," he said.

"Someone stole our dog," Chet explained. "We were out looking for him."

The man scratched his head. "Who are you boys?"

"I'm Chet Morton," Chet replied. "My family owns the farm on top of that ridge." He pointed back the way they'd come. "And these are my friends, Frank and Joe Hardy."

"We'd really appreciate it if you could help us out here, whoever you are," Frank said.

"I'm Leo Myint," the stranger replied. "I run a business out of that factory down there. Let me fetch a shovel from the building."

He trudged back to the factory and returned a few minutes later with a couple of shovels.

"Thanks," Chet said, taking one.

Myint nodded and helped Chet dig the brothers out. "So, who took your dog?" Myint asked.

"Some goons driving snowmobiles," Chet replied. "Seen any around here?"

"I've seen a lot of strangers mucking about the place lately," Myint replied. "They've been buzzing circles around the factory at all hours—day and night. I suspect they're to blame for the troubles

I've had recently—broken windows, missing tools, that kind of thing."

"We've had similar problems at the farm," Chet said.

"Sorry to hear it," Myint said. "This economy is tough enough without burglars and thieves prowling around. Things have been so bad lately, I'm tempted to sell out and move on."

Joe and Frank exchanged a knowing glance, but didn't say anything.

Working with the shovels, Myint and Chet freed the Hardys in a matter of minutes.

"Hey, thanks a lot," Joe said, shaking Myint's hand.

"Don't mention it," Myint replied. "If you don't mind, I'm heading inside before I freeze!"

"Good plan," Frank said. "We're heading for home too."

"I hear some hot cocoa calling me," Chet added, shivering.

"Good luck with your business," Joe said. "What is it you do, by the way?"

"Small plastics manufacturing," Myint said. "Holder trays, bins, that kind of thing. Like I said, though, I'm thinking about selling. Good luck getting home."

"Thanks again," Frank said. Myint hiked back to his factory while Chet and the Hardys slowly climbed upslope to the buggy.

"I was so worried!" Iola said when they finally

reached the top. "I felt helpless waiting up here."

"I'm just glad you weren't caught in the snow-slide," Joe said, giving her a quick hug.

"No sense searching further," Frank said. "The snowfall will have wiped out all the tracks by now."

"We need to get home before we all freeze, anyway," Joe said.

The near-blizzard made it difficult to see, and the howling wind made it impossible to carry on a conversation during the ride home. The teens could barely even hear the chugging of the buggy's four-cylinder engine over the wail of the wind. They drove cautiously through the woods, then skirted a half-dozen farm ponds as they retraced their course back to the barn.

When they finally arrived, all four of them looked more like abominable snowpeople than teenagers. Icicles hung like daggers from the buggy's front and rear bumpers, and the rest of the vehicle looked as though it had been sprayed with thick white frosting.

"This part of the barn isn't too well heated," Chet said, "but the buggy should still melt off pretty quickly." They brushed the snow off the vehicle and dried the engine as best they could, then covered it with the tarp.

"It'll dry out more quickly than we will, I bet," Iola said. "Let's get inside and warm up."

As they walked from the barn to the house, they

spotted an unfamiliar pickup truck in the driveway. The truck was a green late-model vehicle with a small snowplow attached to the front.

The teens took off their soaked snowsuits in the mudroom and went into the kitchen. "Oh, hey, it's J. J.," Chet said, indicating a round-faced, blond-haired man seated at the kitchen table with the Morton grandparents.

Iola introduced the stranger to the Hardys. "J. J. Zuis, these are our friends Joe and Frank Hardy."

The man rose and shook hands with the brothers. "Hi," he said. "John James Zuis—J. J. to my friends. Pleased to meet you." He offered a place at the table where he and the Mortons had just been having coffee. "Take a seat and warm up."

"Land's sake!" Grandma Morton exclaimed. "You all look half frozen. Let me get you some cocoa."

She started to stand, but Joe waved her off. "We can get it," he said. "Standing at a warm stove for a couple of minutes would do us all some good."

The Hardys and their friends made hot chocolate for themselves and warmed up a bit. By the time they sat down at the table to join the conversation, they felt almost human again.

"So, J. J.," Chet said, "what brings you out in this weather?"

"Just checking on your grandparents, Chet," J. J. replied, "making sure they were ready for the big storm. The weather bureau is calling for ten inches or more over the next few days."

"Did you kids have any luck looking for Bernie?" Grandma Morton asked.

"No luck at all," Frank replied. "We saw some snowmobile tracks, but that was about it."

"We met one of your neighbors, too," Joe added. "Leo Myint—he runs a plastic manufacturing business in that old factory."

J. J. nodded. "I met Myint once," he said. "He keeps to himself, pretty much—only has a couple of workers. He tried subletting areas of the factory to other small businesses, but it didn't fly. I think he's the only one left now."

"Patsy Stein's combine has their eye on that land," Grandpa Morton said. "I'm sure she's as eager to buy that old factory as she is to get hold of our farm."

Joe and Frank looked at each other, both thinking along similar lines.

"On a day like today," Grandma said, "I'm half tempted to sell to her. I'm getting too old for blizzards and missing dogs and the like."

J. J. chuckled. "Don't let these two old birds fool you," he said to the Hardys. "They may complain a lot, but they love this place. Mortons have been on this land for five generations, and I expect they'll be here for another five." He stood. "Well, I better be goin'. I've got hatches of my own to batten down. I'll check back in a day or two, make sure everything's all right."

"We appreciate that, J. J.," Grandpa said. "Thanks."

He showed Mr. Zuis to the door, then returned to the table. The Morton family and the Hardys chatted for a while, then they all helped make dinner. The lights flickered as they watched TV afterward, so they broke out the hurricane lanterns, just in case, and built a fire in the fireplace.

The wind howled outside, but they all kept snug and warm, reading beside the crackling blaze.

When the fire burned low, they all decided to turn in. They'd called the police to check about Bernie, but learned nothing new. The storm, it seemed, was keeping the department too busy to look for stray dogs.

The brothers volunteered to clean up when the others went to sleep. They put away the books, gathered all the trash, and finished cleaning the few dishes they'd dirtied since dinnertime. Then both brothers decided to have a glass of warm milk before heading upstairs and changing for bed.

They heated the milk on the stove and sat at the table, sipping from mugs and watching the storm blow outside.

Frank got up to refill their mugs. As he did, Joe said, "I just saw a flashlight outside. There's someone prowling around the barn."

7 Pitched Battle

Frank and Joe put down their mugs and peered out the window. From the kitchen, the brothers had an unobstructed view of the driveway and the barn beyond. Blowing snow, however, made it difficult to see.

"I don't see anything now," Frank said, staring into the stormy darkness. "Do you think it could be the cops?"

"There's no patrol car in the driveway," Joe replied. "And the police wouldn't be poking around at this time of night—especially without telling anyone they were here."

"You're sure about what you saw?"

"Dead certain."

"Let's go check it out."

"Should we tell the Mortons?" Joe asked.

"I'd hate to wake them," Frank said. "They've all had a long day. Besides, for all we know it could just be Bill Backstrom working late."

"In this weather?"

"Maybe not, but still . . . ," Frank said. "I'll suit up while you keep watch, then we'll switch."

Joe nodded and kept looking out the window while Frank donned his snowsuit. Then Frank watched outside while Joe did the same.

"See anything?" Joe asked after he'd finished.

"Maybe a light inside the barn," Frank said. "With the blowing snow, it's hard to tell."

"We'll find out soon enough," Joe said. The brothers zipped up their parkas, pulled on their gloves, and went outside.

The wind howled as they stepped through the back door into the snow. Drifts had piled up across the path, and they had to push their way through the snow just to get to the driveway. Joe turned and said something to Frank, but Frank couldn't hear him above the storm.

"What?" he asked, leaning closer.

"I saw the light again," Joe said. "There's definitely someone in there. I hope it's the dognappers. Wrapping up this case and spending the rest of the night in a warm bed would feel great about now."

Frank nodded his agreement. The two of them

69

trudged forward, moving as quickly as they could without losing their footing on the snow and ice.

They stopped and listened at the barn's double door. The door creaked loudly as Joe put his hooded ear against it.

The younger Hardy grimaced and whispered, "Sorry!"

Frank shrugged. "I don't hear anything," he said. "Let's go in."

They threw the latch, swung the doors open, and hurried inside. The barn was dimly lit. A small compact florescent bulb hanging from a cord near the far wall provided the only illumination. The empty stalls and the hayloft looked weird and eerie in the dim light. Joe pulled the doors shut behind them.

"See anything?" he whispered.

Frank shook his head. The wind outside continued to howl, nearly drowning out the grumblings of the sleepy horses and cows in the barn's rear addition. "Let's look around," the elder Hardy said.

He and Joe moved away from the door, past the thawed-out buggy, and toward the storage bins on either wall. As they did, two intruders jumped from behind the stalls and attacked.

The prowlers were dressed in black snowmobile outfits and wore helmets with ski masks underneath. Each assailant held a pitchfork, apparently taken from a rack against the wall. They jabbed the implements' deadly tines in the direction of the brothers.

Joe stepped back, nearly slipping on the loose hay under his boots. His attacker, who had a red stripe down the middle of his black helmet, threatened his pitchfork at Joe's head.

Frank hopped aside as the second man came at him. The elder Hardy swung his foot in a martial arts block. He kicked the metal head of the pitchfork and the weapon jerked up. The black-helmeted assailant held on, though, and swiped sideways at Frank. Frank stepped back, and the fork's points passed in front of him, mere inches away from his chest.

Joe ducked and Red-Stripe stabbed his pitchfork into a support beam behind the younger Hardy. Joe leaped forward, ramming his shoulder into Red-Stripe's gut. The intruder stumbled backward, letting go of the pitchfork. The weapon remained embedded in the post behind them.

Red-Stripe brought both hands down hard on Joe's back. Joe grunted and fell onto the straw-covered floor. Red-Stripe twisted away from Joe, trying to retrieve the lost pitchfork.

Black-Helmet pushed his fork at Frank again. This time Frank stepped aside and grabbed the shaft of the weapon as it passed.

The elder Hardy twisted hard and wrenched the pitchfork from Black-Helmet's gloved hands.

Black-Helmet seemed surprised for a moment, then he lunged forward and grabbed Frank by the shoulders. He smashed his helmet into the older Hardy's forehead.

Frank reeled back, stunned, still clutching the pitchfork.

Red-Stripe tried to dart past where Joe had fallen. The younger Hardy grabbed the intruder's shoes. Red-Stripe's feet came to a sudden halt, and his momentum toppled him forward. He slammed his helmeted head into the pole next to the pitchfork with a resounding crack. The pitchfork shook loose from the beam and fell beside the trespasser.

Black-Helmet kicked at Frank, but Frank recovered in time to block the blow. The elder Hardy smashed the handle of his pitchfork into the boot of the intruder. Black-Helmet lost his balance and stumbled. Frank lunged forward and thrust the butt end of the pitchfork into Black-Helmet's gut. Black-Helmet exhaled loudly and sat down hard.

Frank stepped forward, still seeing spots from the head butt. He gathered his wits and strength for a final, telling blow.

Red-Stripe's helmet saved him from injury when he cracked his head. He grabbed the pitchfork from the straw-covered floor and got to his feet. Joe leaped at him before he could turn and attack again. The younger Hardy grabbed the weapon by the shaft and the two of them struggled, maneuvering for position, holding the pitchfork crossways between them.

Joe and Red-Stripe spun across the barn like dancers in a deadly waltz. They surged forward and backward, each one unable to see where he was going half the time. Joe nearly forced Red-Stripe into a beam post. Then Red-Stripe heaved and Joe backed hard into Frank, hitting his older brother from behind. Both Hardys went down, but they also managed to hold onto their pitchforks.

Disarmed, Black-Helmet and Red-Stripe bolted for the barn's rear exit. The Hardys scrambled to their feet and gave chase, racing between the animal stalls after the intruders.

The trespassers reached the back door first. They sprinted out and leaped onto waiting snowmobiles. Before the Hardys could catch up, the prowlers fired the engines and roared away into the snowstorm.

"Rats!" Joe snarled. "We'll never catch them on foot! They'll disappear into the darkness before we can do anything."

"Maybe not," Frank said. "Come on!"

He raced back into the main barn with Joe right behind. The younger Hardy paused only long enough to close the rear door to protect the animals from the cold.

The two of them skidded to a halt next to the defrosted buggy. "The headlights will let us see where we're going," Frank said. "Maybe we can still catch them—or at least follow their tracks."

"Check!" Joe said. He opened the main barndoors while Frank threw the tarp into the back seat, started the vehicle, and drove it outside. Then Joe closed the doors and hopped into the passenger seat beside his brother. "Step on it!" he said.

Frank switched on the headlights and roared off into the storm. They cut around behind the barn and quickly picked up the snowmobile tracks. They couldn't see the intruders' taillights, or even hear their quarry over the howl of the wind.

"I guess we didn't hear them arrive because of the storm," Frank said.

"These guys have gotten all the breaks so far," Joe said. "Now its our turn to put the brakes on them."

Frank chuckled. "I just hope that when we catch them, we find out where they took Bernie."

The driving snow made it difficult to see. They were forced to use their low-beam headlights, as the high-beams reflected off the swirling powder, turning the night into a blinding white cloud.

Unfortunately using the low-beams meant they couldn't see very far ahead. Several times Frank swerved at the last moment, barely avoiding a fence or a lone tree standing in the middle of the pasture.

"These bandits know where they're going," Frank

said. "They've easily skirted around obstacles that nearly took us out."

"They're clearly more familiar with these fields than we are," Joe agreed. "Probably they're from nearby."

"Like the Costello farm, for instance?" Frank suggested.

"Maybe," Joe replied. "I was thinking that anyone wanting to buy this farm would probably become pretty familiar with its layout."

"So Patsy Stein's mall consortium is at the top of your suspects list," Frank said.

"It wouldn't be the first time a criminal has tried to force owners off their land," Joe concluded.

The buggy left the pasture and zipped through the stand of pine trees that stretched down from the northern forest. The snow grew worse by the minute, limiting visibility even further.

"I think I see their taillights!" Joe said, pointing through the trees.

Frank nodded and smiled, but just at that moment, the buggy's headlights flickered. "It must be a loose wire!" the elder Hardy said.

"We don't have time to fix it," Joe countered. "If we do, we'll lose them for sure. And the way this snow is blowing, we might lose their tracks as well."

The woods gave way to pasture again as the intruders turned south. Snowdrifts sprang up suddenly across the snowmobile tracks. The Hardys plowed forward without slowing down. The powdery obstacles burst into blinding clouds as the buggy rushed through.

"We're off course," Frank said after a particularly bad whiteout. The bandits rode on their right now, rather than ahead of them.

"They could be cutting back toward the main road," Joe said, nearly shouting to be heard above the storm and the growl of the buggy's engine.

"I'll cut across the field and try to head them off," Frank said. He turned to the right, angling the vehicle over a patch of clear snow separating them from the intruders. The buggy's headlights flickered again, but the brothers were too intent on catching their foes to worry about it.

"We're catching up!" Joe exclaimed. Then his blue eyes went wide. "Frank! Watch out for that—!"

Before he could finish, they burst through another drift and skidded onto a large farm pond. The ice beneath the vehicle gave way, and the buggy pitched into the cold, dark water.

8 Frozen Stiffs

The chilly liquid burst up all around the Hardys, spraying into their eyes and over their clothing.

The buggy came to a sudden, violent halt, half-submerged in the pond. Frank and Joe jerked forward in their seats; only their seat belts kept them from flying over the stripped-down vehicle's hood.

"Are you okay?" Frank asked.

"Aside from being soaked, you mean?" Joe replied. "Yeah."

The buggy's rear-mounted engine remained above the water and was still running. The drive wheels, also in the rear, were tipped up at an angle and had nothing to purchase on. The tires spun wildly through the snowy air while the engine roared. Frank switched off the engine and pocketed the key.

With broken ice and chilly water pressing in around them, it took the brothers a few minutes to struggle out of their seat belts. Then they crawled through the marshy, half-frozen edge of the pond back onto the snow-covered pasture.

Joe gazed at the half-submerged buggy. "Think there's any chance we could pull it out?" he asked.

Frank shook his head. "Not tonight—not before we freeze, anyway." He grabbed the tarp from the back seat and threw it over the engine to protect it. "What about using the rope? We could run the rope to a tree and drag it out."

"The rope's in the trunk, and the trunk's in front—underwater," Frank replied. "So unless you feel like ice diving . . ."

"Not without a wet suit."

"Let's go," Frank said. "It's not getting any warmer. Got your flashlight?"

Joe fished a penlight out of one of his coat pockets and switched it on. "Still works," he said.

"Good," said Frank. "We'll follow the tracks back as far as we can. Hopefully we'll spot the house before the trail drifts over."

"If we don't, I guess the Mortons will be able to use us as lawn ornaments until we thaw out in the spring," Joe said sardonically.

Frank chuckled, but he was already beginning to

feel chilled. Their waterproof parkas had protected the brothers' torsos some, but the rest of them was still pretty soaked. "We'd better get moving before we freeze in place," Frank said. He and Joe trudged back through the snow along the tire tracks.

The heavy snowfall made the landscape gray and surreal. Pale light reflected from everywhere. Most of the time, they didn't even need the flashlight to see.

"It'd be beautiful if I weren't freezing," Joe said.

"We'd turn into Popsicles before we could build a decent fire," Frank said. "If we keep moving as fast as we can, our body heat should dry off some of the water."

Joe nodded and the two began jogging through the rising drifts.

They stopped briefly to catch their breath under the shelter of the south-reaching spur of pines. They didn't stay long, though. Frank's plan to warm up by running had worked, but their clothes began to freeze again almost as soon as they stopped. In addition both brothers knew the weather conditions were worsening every moment they delayed.

Driving winds and blowing snow made it nearly impossible to follow the buggy tracks once they left the forest. Fortunately both brothers had wilderness scout training, so they had a pretty a good idea where the Morton farmhouse lay, even if they couldn't see it.

They forged ahead, moving as quickly as they could, plowing through the growing snowdrifts. They avoided several farm ponds: wide, flat expanses of snow-covered, treacherous ice. Ahead, solitary hedge evergreens poked up through the drifts like pointy-hatted sentries trying to block the brothers' way.

Taking shelter from the wind behind one of the larger trees, the Hardys took a moment to catch their breaths and reorient themselves. As they did, Joe's flashlight went dark.

"The water must have shorted it out," he said. "I just put in new batteries."

"Don't worry," Frank said. "We can't be far from the house now."

"I hope not," Joe replied, shivering. "I don't know how much longer I can keep going."

"We'll walk as long as we need to," Frank said. "I'd hate to come this far only to freeze to death within site of the barn."

But they couldn't see the barn or the house from where they were. The rolling pasture and blizzard conditions made every direction look the same. They steeled themselves and forged on.

Their lungs began to burn from the cold. Their legs felt as though icy needles poked them at every step. Joe stumbled and fell face-first into a drift.

Frank pulled him up again, but he seemed exhausted too.

"M-maybe we sh-should have built that f-fire instead," Joe said.

"T-too late . . . n-now," Frank replied.

A row of wild hedge pines rose up before them, attempting to trap the brothers in the deadly winter wonderland. The Hardys staggered to the trees and leaned against the trunks, trying to rally, trying to muster the strength to continue. Joe pressed his face to the cold, snow-covered branches. Incongruously, they felt warm to him.

Joe had heard that feeling warm was a sign of hypothermia. Your body gets so cold it can't tell it's freezing anymore. He longed to close his eyes and rest, just for a minute.

The trees shuddered and Joe realized without looking that Frank must have collapsed.

The younger Hardy forced his eyes open and peered through the pine needles at his brother lying in the snow. Something glistening in the distance caught his eye.

"A light!" he cried. "I see the house!"

He grabbed Frank's shoulder and shook it. "I see it!" he repeated. "We're almost home!"

Wearily, Frank opened his eyes. Ice and snow crusted his eyelashes and eyebrows. He looked more frozen than alive.

Joe helped his older brother to stand, and they leaned against each other. Together, they staggered through the drifts toward the beckoning lights. It

81

took them nearly fifteen minutes to cross the remaining three hundred yards to the house.

Exhausted, they wrenched the back door open, and stumbled inside.

"Joe! Frank!" Iola cried. Worry filled her pretty voice.

The brothers were picked up by warm hands and steered into chairs by the stove. The old cookstove was warm and had coffee and cocoa simmering on a burner.

The Hardys stripped off their freezing clothes while the Mortons wrapped them in blankets. Grandpa brought buckets of tepid water to warm the Hardys' feet while Grandma plied them with cocoa.

An hour later, the brothers felt much better.

"Thanks for all your help," Frank said sleepily.

"If you hadn't been up," Joe added, "you might have found us passed out on the kitchen floor come morning." He yawned.

"The back door slamming woke us," Grandpa said. "Then we spotted a commotion out by the barn. Before we could get dressed to help you, we saw you boys drive off into the snowstorm."

"Not your brightest move ever," Chet noted.

"Where's the buggy?" Iola asked.

Frank shook his head ruefully. "We got blinded by the storm and drove it into a pond."

"No wonder you were soaked!" Iola exclaimed.

"It's swamped but not completely sunk," Joe said. He looked at the Morton grandparents and added, "We're *so* sorry. We'll drag it out tomorrow if we can."

"We'll fix any damage, too," Frank added.

"Now, don't you worry about that," Grandpa Morton countered. "What's done is done."

"Eat this," Grandma said, handing each Hardy a bowl of homemade chicken soup.

Joe and Frank ate the soup gratefully, feeling more and more like their old selves with every passing minute.

As the Mortons bustled about, busy with other tasks, Joe looked at Frank.

"We really blew this one," he whispered. "Not only did we lose the bad guys, but we sank the buggy as well."

Frank nodded grimly. "We've got a lot to make up for. We can't let the Mortons down again."

By mid morning, the snow had subsided, though it didn't let up entirely. Plows cleared Kendall Ridge Road and, aside from Bernie being missing, life at the farm returned to its winter routine.

The Hardys slept in late, recovering from their ordeal. They woke feeling achy and cramped, but still much better than they had the previous night.

If the Mortons felt angry about the brothers driving the buggy into the pond, none of them showed it when the Hardys came down for a very late breakfast. Grandpa happily served the brothers ham and eggs, while Iola brought toast and juice. Chet kept busy washing the dishes, and Grandma returned to housecleaning.

The normality of the whole routine made Frank and Joe feel even more guilty. The Mortons were good people, and certainly didn't need the added grief that the Hardys had inadvertently caused.

"You missed quite a parade of well-wishers this morning," Chet commented as the brothers ate.

"Oh?" Joe asked.

"J. J. stopped by," Iola said, picking up her brother's train of thought. "So did Patsy Stein and Gail Sanchez."

"What did they want?" Frank asked.

"The usual," Grandpa replied. "J. J. was just checkin' in on us. Sanchez came by to try and pawn off some of her 'top of the line' snow removal equipment. And Stein's still making insulting offers to buy the farm."

"I guess she figures if she pesters you enough, you might give in," Joe said.

Grandpa paused and stretched, as though his back were aching. "Sometimes this farm does seem more trouble than it's worth," he admitted, "but I don't really think that Bayport needs another mall no matter how top-class it is." He shot the teenagers a half smile.

"Mr. Myint doesn't agree, apparently," Iola said. "Ms. Stein said he's already signed aboard her plan."

Grandpa harrumphed. "Just because Patsy Stein says something, doesn't make it true."

Joe and Frank glanced at each other, each wondering about Stein's connection to the farm's troubles.

"Maybe we can drag the buggy out of the pond today," Frank suggested.

"Don't you worry about that," Grandma said, poking her head in from the other room. "We don't want you straining yourselves after your close call last night."

"We'd really feel better if we brought it home," Joe said.

Grandma shook her head. "I won't hear of it. I don't want either of you gettin' sick over that old piece of junk. A day or two in the ice won't hurt it. You two take it easy today."

Reluctantly, Joe and Frank nodded. "Yeah, okay," Joe said.

"Good," Grandpa said. "With Chet and Iola's help, even if Bill's snowed in, I think we can manage all the chores around this place. You two relax and recover."

"If you're really itching to do something," Grandma added, "turn your brains on figuring out who took Bernie."

"No news from the police?" Frank asked.

"We called 'em, but they didn't have anything new," Grandpa replied.

"We'll see what we can do, then," Joe promised.

He and Frank finished their breakfast while the Mortons went about their chores. After cleaning up, the brothers donned their snow gear—which Grandma had run through the dryer while they slept—and headed back outside.

"Looks like it's foot patrol for us today," Joe said.

"After nearly freezing last night, stretching our legs will probably do us good," Frank replied. "At least it's warmer out today than it was last night."

"And not so snowy," Joe agreed. "I don't think Grandma Morton would mind us taking a walk. Where do you want to start?"

"That spur of pine woods to the east," Frank suggested. "We know the snowmobilers went through there. Maybe we can pick up their tracks."

"That's a pretty good hike," Joe replied.

Frank smiled wryly. "Think of it as penance," he said.

On their way to the forest, they walked past the pond where they'd swamped the buggy. Both brothers felt relieved that there didn't seem to be much damage, aside from the fact that the vehicle's nose was wedged into the water. The temperature was hovering around freezing, and little ice had reformed where the buggy broke through.

"Maybe we should pull it out anyway," Joe suggested.

Frank shook his head. "The Mortons told us not to," he replied. "They're not mad at us right now, but if we broke Grandma's 'orders' they might be."

Joe reluctantly agreed, and the two continued on to the south-reaching spur of the big pine forest. Inside the woods, it didn't take them long to discover snowmobile tracks peeking out amid the drifts.

"Hey," Frank said, "check this out. There are some dog prints next to these snowmobile tracks over here."

"Do you think they might be from Bernie?" Joe asked.

"Could be," Frank replied. "They look big enough."

"The dog track is on top of the tread impression," Joe said. "So the dog was here *after* the snowmobile. Could Bernie have escaped?"

Frank shrugged. "Let's follow the tracks and see where they lead," he suggested.

The brothers trudged through the woods for ten minutes, heading north toward the power lines. They nearly lost the trail a few times, but finally reached the edge of the forest.

Joe scratched his head. "Okay," he said, "I think we're on the wrong track." He stooped to examine a patch of tracks on the ground. "It looks like there's more than one dog here."

"I think that's a reasonable assumption," Frank said, his voice suddenly filled with tension.

Joe looked up just as a loud growling shattered the stillness of the snowy winter air.

At the edge of the woods on the other side of the power lines prowled a pack of angry-looking dogs. And as soon as the canines spotted the brothers, they charged.

9 Snow-Dog Days

The pack ran directly for the Hardys, bounding across the treeless swath surrounding the power lines. Savage barks and angry howls cut through the chilly afternoon air.

"Run!" Frank cried.

The brothers turned and sprinted back toward the forest. They had a sixty-yard head start on the pack, and both Frank and Joe were good runners. The snow slowed them down, though, and even the fastest human sprinter couldn't outrun swift dogs like these for long.

Joe glanced back as they ran, sizing up their pursuers. "I see six," he told Frank. "Two are huskies, two look like shepherd mixes, and two are mutts."

"That's a pretty odd pack for a bunch of wild dogs,"

89

Frank said, not slowing down as they conversed.

"You're thinking someone set them on us?"

"Maybe. Did you see any collars?"

"I wasn't looking that close," Joe replied. "You can stop and check for tags if you like."

"No thanks," Frank said. "We may get a better look soon anyway." He smiled ruefully.

"I'd give about anything for a good set of skis right now," Joe said.

"Why don't you wish us up a snowmobile instead," Frank suggested. Both brothers kept their tones light, though each realized the graveness of their situation. Caught in the wilderness with no weapons, if they were caught by the pack, they stood little chance.

The snarls and barks of the dogs grew louder.

"They're gaining on us," Frank said, daring a backward glance.

"Up into the trees," Joe suggested. "It's our only hope."

Both brothers headed for the nearest climbable pines. They picked separate trees, not wanting to chance their combined weight on just one. They scrambled up into the low-hanging branches as swiftly as squirrels. The dogs leaped after them, snapping at their heels. The brothers shinnied up the trunks, out of reach.

"Well," Joe said, panting, "that was . . . stimulating."

He clung precariously to the branches of a big white pine.

"Not something I plan to do every day," Frank commented. He sat perched in a similar tree, about five yards away from his brother. Powdery snow drifted down from the branches above him, chilling the older Hardy's face.

The stray dogs circled around the trees, howling and barking, looking up hungrily at the brothers.

"Do you have the cell phone?" Frank asked.

Joe nodded. "I stuffed it into my pocket before we went out, just in case." He fished the phone out of his parka, pressed a few buttons, and then frowned. "Nothing!" he said, frustrated. "I can't get a signal."

"Maybe it's interference from the electric towers," Frank suggested. "Or maybe the farm is in one of those cell phone 'dead zones.'"

"Either way, we're up a tree, literally and figuratively," Joe said, putting the phone away. "Maybe we can throw some pinecones at them, scare them off."

"It's worth a try," he said. "I don't have a better idea, at any rate."

The brothers inched higher up their trees until they could reach clusters of big pinecones dangling overhead. When they'd collected enough ammunition, they took aim at the pack circling below.

"Try for their noses," Frank said. "If we can give them a good enough sting, maybe they'll back off."

They pelted the dogs with pinecones for several minutes, scoring a few hits and being rewarded with several yelps. The pack wasn't discouraged, though. The dogs quickly became wise to the brothers' tactics and scurried back, out of easy range, while continuing to circle the trees from a safe distance.

"I suppose we could try lighting the pinecones on fire," Joe said, feeling frustrated.

"Too tricky," Frank said, shaking his head. "Climbing down and brandishing lit branches might work, though. A makeshift torch would at least keep them at bay."

"Or we could try to wait them out," Joe replied. "We're well-clothed, well-fed, and dry. It's not like we're going to perish any time soon."

Frank glanced up through the branches at the gray winter sky and the blowing snow. "The storm's building," he said. "If we stay here too long, we'll be blundering back to the farm in a snowstorm again—assuming the dogs leave at all."

"All right," Joe said. "The flaming branch idea is worth a shot. Do you have any matches?"

"I was an Eagle Scout," Frank replied. "I *always* have matches."

The brothers climbed lower, searching out dead branches to make torches with. They had their pocketknives as well as matches and soon selected a few good limbs to make into firebrands.

As Joe was cutting through his branch, though, the treelimb under him creaked loudly and then snapped.

"Joe!" Frank shouted as his brother fell.

Joe reached out and grabbed a smaller branch nearby, but it snapped under his weight as well. He grabbed at another, and then another. The third held, though it groaned at supporting him.

The younger Hardy clung desperately to the limb, his boots dangling two yards above the forest floor. The pack of dogs raced under the hapless teen, jumping and trying to bite his toes.

"Hang on, Joe!" Frank said. His gloved fingers fumbled with his matches as he tried desperately to light the branch he was holding.

Slowly, Joe edged down the dangling limb toward the tree trunk, hoping to climb up once more.

Frank lit his makeshift torch, but dropped the book of matches as he did so. The matches tumbled into the savage pack below.

"Shoo! Go home!" Frank shouted futilely. He leaned down from his perch, waving the burning stick at the dogs.

But with Joe dangling just out of reach, the pack showed no intention of leaving. They barked and snapped and redoubled their efforts.

Joe had almost reached his tree's main trunk

now, but the branch he was clinging to groaned more loudly with every passing second.

Frank clenched his teeth, preparing to jump down and fight the dogs if his brother fell.

A shrill whistle sounded, cutting through the winter wind, keening above the snarls of the pack. Instantly, the dogs all stopped running and barking. They turned their heads toward the north and listened.

Joe seized upon the momentary reprieve. He swung back onto the main trunk just as his branch gave way. He shinnied up higher, out of reach of the dogs. Frank breathed a long sigh of relief.

"What was that sound?" Joe asked.

Frank shrugged, concentrating on keeping his torch alight in case they still needed it.

"Who's up there?" a gruff voice called. "Show yourselves! You can't escape!"

"We're not trying to escape," Joe called. "We're just trying to keep out of reach of these dogs!"

Vic Costello, dressed in a blaze-orange jacket, stepped into view. He carried a shotgun in one hand and a metal whistle in the other. His eyes narrowed. "I shoulda known it'd be some of you Morton kids setting my dogs loose from their pen!" he growled. "I ought to blast you just on principle!"

"We didn't set them loose," Joe shot back. "We were walking toward the power lines when they rushed out of the woods and attacked us."

Frank kept hold of his emotions. "If we had set your dogs free," he said reasonably, "don't you think we'd have had a better plan to get away than running up a tree?"

Costello stuffed the whistle into his vest pocket. "I did see snowmobile tracks near the pen," he said. "And you'd have to be pretty dim—even for a Morton—to get off a machine after opening the kennel door." He looked around, as if expecting to find a snowmobile hidden nearby. When he didn't see one, he called to the dogs, "Come here, boys! Sit! Let those varmints out of the trees."

The dogs trotted over and sat down beside Costello, though they continued glaring at the Hardys.

"Thanks," Frank said. He and his brother swung quickly down to the snow-covered forest floor. Frank extinguished his firebrand and picked up his lost matches.

"Are you sure you didn't leave the dog pen unlocked?" Joe asked.

"Fine way to thank a man for savin' your life," Costello scoffed. "Only a spoiled boy would ask that kind of question. Out here, our animals are our lives. We're very careful with them." He turned and, motioning to the pack, walked back toward the power lines.

"Where are you going?" Joe asked.

"Home," Costello replied. "You don't think I

want to stay on Morton land any longer than I need to, do ya?"

"Thanks again," Frank said as Costello tramped off. The farmer didn't reply, though his dogs continued to shoot hungry glances toward the brothers as Vic and the pack disappeared back into the woods.

"That was lucky, him coming along when he did," Joe said.

"If luck had anything to do with it," Frank replied.

Joe's blue eyes narrowed. "You think he might have let the dogs free on purpose?"

"I can't rule it out," Frank said. "Doing so would give him a good excuse to prowl around the Morton property—and maybe cause a bit of mischief himself. We have only his word about those snowmobile tracks."

"That's true," Joe said, "and I doubt we'll be visiting his farm to corroborate the story."

"With the way this storm is picking up," Frank said, "I don't think we'd get the chance, even if he and the Mortons were best friends. Come on, let's get back before we turn into snowmen."

Joe nodded, and he and Frank slogged back to the Morton farm through the escalating snow.

By the time they returned to the old farmhouse, the storm had reached blizzard proportions. They could barely see twenty yards in any direction through the blowing snow.

They met Chet and Iola returning from the barn.

"Boy, are we glad to see you guys," Chet said as they all headed for the house.

"We were starting to get worried," Iola added.

"We spotted some dog tracks in the woods," Joe explained. "We thought they might be Bernie's, but it turned out they belonged to a pack owned by Vic Costello."

"Costello said someone set the dogs loose from his kennels," Frank added.

"Do you think it could have been the same person that took Bernie?" Iola asked.

"Might be," Joe said.

They took off their snow gear in the mudroom and went into the kitchen. Just as they got inside, the power flickered and then went out.

"That's been happening all afternoon," Chet said. Gray, ghostly light from the snow blowing outside filtered through the old house's windows. The Mortons had been busy while the Hardys were gone; all the windows in the house were now covered with clear insulating plastic.

"Usually the lights came right back on, though," Iola added. "Maybe this time they're out for good."

The phone rang, and a minute later Grandma Morton came into the kitchen. "That was J. J. Zuis," she said. "Some fool hit a telephone pole up the highway. The power's out in this whole area until they can get a crew to repair it."

"Which, in this weather, might not be any time soon," Grandpa Morton added as he entered the room. "You Hardy boys have a nice walk?"

Joe and Frank glanced at each other, then said, "Yes." It seemed easier not to go into details of their adventure right at that moment.

"Let's get some lamps lit and the fire going," Grandpa said. "It'll be dark soon, and even with the plastic on the windows, this old house still leaks heat like a sieve."

They all did as Grandpa suggested. Then the Hardys went out to the old water tower and filled up buckets with fresh water. The tower's foam insulation kept it from freezing for most of the winter.

"There's an old pump back near the horses that'll keep the animals in good stead," Grandpa told the brothers as they returned. "Us, too, if the tower runs low. Its a long haul from there to the house, though."

With their preparations to weather the storm finished, there was nothing to do but sit by the fire and enjoy "roughing it." They could light the stove by hand, so there was still plenty of hot food and drinks to go around. They warmed up the remainder of Grandma Morton's chicken soup for dinner and ate by candlelight. Then they snacked on cookies and played games by the fire. Frank came dangerously close to beating Grandpa Morton at chess. In the end, though, the elder Hardy had to concede defeat.

The wind howled loudly around the drafty old house, reminding Frank and Joe of the baying of the dogs circling their pine trees earlier in the day.

Chet got up and stretched. "I'm grabbing some more cocoa," he said. "Anyone want some?"

Everyone did, and his grandparents wanted more coffee. "I'll help you carry the mugs," Frank said, rising and following Chet into the kitchen.

The two puttered around the stove, preparing the drinks. Frank fetched everyone's mugs from the living room so they could refill them. As he returned to the kitchen, he found Chet staring out the window overlooking the backyard.

Frank stopped beside his friend and followed Chet's gaze.

Chet gasped. "Fire!"

10 The Long, Hot Winter

Yellow flames licked up the side of the red barn. They weren't very big, but they were growing rapidly.

"Fire!" Frank yelled. He dropped the mugs on the table and followed Chet out the rear door. They paused only long enough to grab their parkas and put them on as they rushed outside. Joe dashed out a moment later, just behind his brother. The rest of the Mortons followed.

"We'll take care of the animals!" Grandma cried, hurrying around the barn toward the pens with Iola.

Grandpa threw a garden hose from the main house to Joe, then went to turn it on. "There may not be much pressure left 'cause the electricity is out," he said. "If it fails, we can hook a line to the water tower."

Joe ran to where Chet and Frank were throwing

snow on the fire. He opened up the hose's nozzle. For a minute water sputtered out of the hose, stanching the flames a bit. Then, just as Grandpa had predicted, the pressure gave out.

"Maybe I'll invest in a generator next year," Grandpa Morton said ruefully.

Frank and Chet had run to the nearby water tower as Joe used the garden hose. Chet threw open a wooden bin that had been sheltered by the aging structure's stout legs. "There's an old fire hose in here," he said. "They only use it for filling up water trucks to take to the field, so it doesn't have a great nozzle on it."

"With luck, it'll be good enough," Frank said.

As the garden hose drizzled out, Joe came and helped Frank and Chet hook up the water tower to the old fire hose. The Hardys lugged the heavy tubing toward the fire while Chet connected the end to the water tower tap and prepared to turn on the spigot.

Grandpa fetched a blanket out of the back of the station wagon and tried to beat the flames down. But the fire had climbed up higher than he could reach.

"Let 'er rip!" Frank called as they came within range of the burning barn wall.

Chet twisted the valve on the water tank spigot and water shot through the hose and out of the nozzle. Chet had been right; the nozzle wasn't very good and as much water squirted out the sides as the front. Frank and Joe fought to direct the spray toward the burning wall.

The water pressure from the tower left a lot to be desired, though it was better than they'd gotten from the fire hose. Fortunately the weather was with them. The wind and snow seemed to be taking a breather. None of the group believed that would last, though.

As they worked frantically to extinguish the blaze, two pickup trucks skidded into the driveway, coming to a halt near the back door. Bill Backstrom and J. J. Zuis leaped from their vehicles and ran to help the Mortons and their friends. They grabbed some buckets from beneath the water tower and filled them from the wild spray sloshing out of the old fire hose.

"Glad you two dropped by," Grandpa said as he gave up on the blanket and fetched a bucket for himself.

"I was heading home from town when I saw the light and you folks running around out here," Backstrom replied.

"I spotted the fire while working in the fields near my place," J. J. added. "With the power out, this blaze is the brightest spot for miles around. If the storm hadn't cleared a bit, though, I never would have seen it."

"Whatever the reasons you came," Chet said, "we're glad you showed up to help." He grabbed a bucket of his own and joined the brigade.

"Did either of you call the fire department?" Frank asked.

Both Backstrom and Zuis shook their heads. "I tried, but the phones were out at my place," J. J. said. "And I don't have a cell phone."

"Me either," admitted Backstrom.

"Cell phone!" Joe said, slapping his forehead. He let Frank handle the old hose, got out of side-splatter range, and pulled the phone out of his pocket. He punched 9-1-1, then listened. "Rats. Nothing!"

"Service is pretty bad out here," J. J. explained. He sloshed another bucket of stray water onto the fire. "That's why I don't have a cell phone."

"They're talking about putting a cell tower in that new mall complex they want to build," Backstrom added.

"Well, that ain't gonna help us now," Grandpa said. "Keep bailing!"

Between the Hardys, the Mortons, and the two volunteers, they soon brought the blaze under control. The wall of the old barn was badly scorched in places, but not entirely burned through.

The impromptu firefighters breathed a collective sigh of relief. Chet twisted the aging water tower's spigot closed. The storm began to build again. The wind picked up and fresh drifts snaked across the driveway.

"Thank you, each and every one," Grandpa said. "We might have lost the barn without you."

"What are neighbors for?" J. J. asked rhetorically.

"Hey," Bill Backstrom said jovially, "I was just savin' my own job. I certainly don't want to be lookin' to Stein's mall for work, and J. J.'s not hiring." He smiled at farmer Zuis.

J. J. shook his head. "I think the Mortons need you here, Bill." Both of the men chuckled.

"You smell that?" Joe asked, sniffing the air. "Smells like gasoline."

"You didn't leave one of our gas cans near that side of the barn while you were working, did you Bill?" Grandpa Morton asked.

"Not me," Backstrom replied. "I haven't touched the can since I worked on the tractor the other day."

"If the phones are working inside the house, we should call the fire department and have them check it out," Frank said. "It looks like arson to me."

Grandma Morton and Iola came around the side of the barn, dusting hay and snow off of their clothes. "Call in more people? Tonight? In this weather?" Grandma said. "It looks to me like we've got this under control. Let the professionals go where they're really needed . . . or stay at home—which is where all sensible people should be tonight."

"We got all the animals safely outside," Iola said, "just in time to move them back, I guess." She sighed.

"Better to be safe than sorry," Grandpa said.

"Don't worry," J. J. added, "we'll help you get them back inside."

He and the rest went to help relocate the animals and bed them down for the night. Grandma Morton and Iola coordinated the effort, and soon the rear of the barn was full of the sounds of contented horses and cows once more.

"I think it's time for more cocoa," Chet said.

"My grandson's right," Grandpa agreed. "Coffee and cocoa for everyone."

J. J. Zuis and Bill Backstrom looked around at the escalating snow. "Thanks, Dave," J. J. said, "but I think I better be getting home."

"Me too, boss," Backstrom said. "This storm is getting pretty nasty. Like Marge said, all sensible people should be safe at home tonight."

"We'll take a 'snow check' though," J. J. added, smiling.

"You could stay the night if you like," Grandma suggested. "We've got plenty of blankets and space. It'd be safer to go home in the morning, probably."

"No, thank you, Marge," J. J. said.

"I really have to go too," Backstrom added. "Gotta feed my dog."

"Suit yourselves," Grandpa replied. "Can't say I blame you. Drive safely."

J. J. and Backstrom said their good-byes, got back in their trucks, and headed off into the storm.

"They don't have far to go," Grandma said, watching them drive away. "They should be all right."

The Mortons and the Hardys tidied up as best they could around the barn. The side where they'd been fighting the fire was all ice and rapidly freezing slush.

"You all watch your steps around here for the next few days," Grandpa cautioned. "I don't want anyone slipping and breaking their neck."

The storm grew even worse as they shoveled slush, and the group was soon forced to retreat back into the farmhouse. They stripped off their sopping wet gear in the mudroom at the back door, then went to warm themselves by the fire.

Iola and Joe put themselves in charge of the hot beverages and took turns ferrying drinks from the kitchen to the living room. Soon everyone was feeling toasty and warm once more. Grandma set up an old-fashioned wooden drying rack near the fire. Frank brought in their wet clothing and hung them up to dry.

Fighting the fire had drained most of the energy from the Morton grandparents. Dave and Marge Morton retired early, first making sure all the teenagers had extra blankets to keep warm during the night.

Joe and Frank decided to sleep in the living

room. Their room on the second floor was far enough away from the fireplaces to be pretty chilly.

"I'd rather wake up with a stiff neck from sleeping on the couch than a stiff body from freezing," Joe joked.

The rooms Iola and Chet had were warmer because they were closer to the central chimney. The Morton teens turned in not long after their grandparents.

Outside, the wind howled relentlessly and the snow began to climb higher up the clapboards of the old farmhouse.

Frank and Joe sat by the fire, listening to the storm and thinking about the troubles at the farm.

"I'm betting the fire was the work of those guys who jumped us last night," Joe said.

"Hit-and-run does seem to be their M.O.," Frank agreed. "And the smell of gasoline around the fire seems to rule out any kind of an accident. The question remains, though, who's behind it all?"

"Backstrom and J. J. Zuis came to help," Joe said, "but they could still be in on it. They've known the Mortons a long time. Maybe there's some kind of grudge there. Plus, they arrived awfully fast. Maybe one of them set the fire to begin with."

"Maybe," Frank said, "though they could just have spotted the blaze like they said. I'm leaning toward the Costellos right now. There are two of them, and they definitely don't seem to like the

Mortons. We have only Mr. Costello's word that someone else let his dogs loose."

"It could be he was covering up for kidnapping Bernie," Joe suggested, "making it seem like dog troubles were widespread in the area."

"Gail Sanchez or Patsy Stein might be responsible too," Frank said.

Joe nodded. "Trouble at the farm could mean more business for Sanchez's farm supply outfit. And we know that Stein wants to buy up this place, along with other properties in the area. She's already got her eye on the Myint factory."

"Malls need a lot of space," Frank admitted.

"I'm with the Mortons, though," Joe replied. "Bayport doesn't need another mall."

A sudden thud outside brought both brothers to the window.

After taking a look, Joe breathed a sigh of relief. "It was just a big pile of snow that slipped off the roof," he said.

"We'll probably hear a lot of sounds like that before the night's over," Frank said. "Look at the way the snow is piling up! There must be five inches more since we came inside."

"Its a regular blizzard, all right," Joe agreed. "We're lucky to be in here, not still trapped up in those trees."

"I'm just hoping we've seen the last of our troubles for the night," Frank said.

"You'd have to be a pretty determined criminal to venture out in this kind of snow," Joe replied.

"I think it's safe to say that the people causing these problems—whoever they are—are pretty determined," Frank said.

"You know, it occurs to me," Joe said, "if anything else goes wrong before this blows over, we'll be on our own. There's no way fire and rescue or even the police, could get out here to help. You'd have to call in the National Guard to plow through this weather."

"And it'd be pretty hard to call the guard with the phones out," Frank added.

"And the cell phone on the fritz," Joe finished.

Frank looked grim. "Face it," he said in a low voice, "as of now, we're completely on our own. It's you, me, and the Morton family against the people behind this trouble. Every one of us is trapped in this blizzard with no way out."

11 Stranded in the Snow

Neither Frank nor Joe slept well that night. It seemed they woke up every thirty minutes or so to check on some new noise—whether real or imagined. Nothing came of any of the noises, and when morning finally arrived, all they had to show for their lonely vigil was bags under their eyes.

Dawn broke in muted tones of gray and white. Snow was still falling, though less fiercely than it had during the night. The wind had quieted some as well, after pushing drifts up to the windowsills on the west side of the house.

The old farmhouse was chilly inside, and everyone came to the living room wrapped in blankets, pajamas, and robes. Frank and Joe soon got the fire stoked up. Then they volunteered to put on their dry snow gear and fetch more wood from the shed out back.

They had to push the back door through a snow drift to get it open. Bernie's doghouse lay completely buried; only a vague bulge in the blanket of snow showed where it stood.

While the Hardys fetched wood, the Mortons fired up the kitchen and made breakfast. Pancakes, ham, eggs, and hash browns were the order of the day. "A body needs lots of fuel to fight this kind of cold and hardship," Grandpa Morton explained.

"Can't argue with you there," Joe said, wolfing down his second helping.

"There's at least a foot of snow outside," Frank said. "More in the drifts. One came up above my waist."

"I remember about thirty years ago, we got close to three feet of snow in a day and a half," Grandma said. "Shut down the whole state for a week. They had to call out the National Guard to clear the roads and ferry sick folks to hospitals on snowmobiles. We didn't have power for six days."

"Let's hope it's not that bad this time!" Chet said.

"Don't worry," Grandpa replied. "They've got better equipment now than we did then. They'll have this cleared up in a couple of days, I expect."

"The food in the fridge might go bad before the power comes back," Iola noted.

"Why do we need a fridge with all this ice and

snow around?" Grandma asked. "We'll just transfer the perishables out of the fridge into the mudroom."

"Good idea, Ma," Grandpa said. "The back hall ain't heated, and we've got that storage bin we could keep things in."

"Sounds like our next project," Frank said.

"You boys can help Grandma take care of it," Grandpa said. "Iola and I will go tend to the animals, *after* I have another helping of these excellent hash browns."

Chet smiled. "Gramps is right, Grandma. You've done it again." He reached his plate out for seconds as well.

Cleaning up the dishes had to wait until the boys carried in water, so they bused the dishes to the sink and then tackled their chores after eating. It didn't take the brothers and Chet long to help Grandma empty out the fridge. They put all the food in the big storage box near the bench where they changed into their snowsuits, while Grandpa and Iola fed the horses and cows.

Soon the teenagers all went out and ferried in buckets of water from the rusting water tower. They filled up the first floor bathtub as a reserve supply and topped off all the clean pots and jugs they could find. Then they filled a big kettle on the stove to boil warm water for the dishes.

"Thank goodness winter storms can't drag down the gas lines!" Grandpa joked.

"It's like the old days, isn't it, Pa?" Grandma said. "Before everything got so fancy and electrified."

"It's kind of romantic, really," Iola noted. "Getting warm by a fire, hauling the water, cooking by candlelight. Some people pay good money for a 'get away from it all' vacation—and here we are at home in Bayport having the same experience."

"I kind of doubt that your mom and dad would trade their cruise for this," Joe said, smiling.

Iola laughed. "Trade lounging on a secluded beach for hauling water through the snow?" she said. "No, I doubt they would."

"Personally, I'll take the electricity every day of the week, Iola," Grandpa said. "All this strain and exercise might be fine for you young people, but I'm getting too old for it. It'll probably take a week for my back to recover from this 'fun.'"

"We'll try to handle all the back-breaking work, Mr. Morton," Frank said. "Just point us in the right direction."

"All right, young man," Grandpa replied, "next on the list is to go out to the barn and patch that wall a bit. It may not have burned clear through, but I bet it's even draftier inside than usual. Our animals would appreciate keeping whatever warmth their enclosure's got."

"Chet, you can fetch the snowblower out of the barn and clear the drive and walkways," Grandma said.

"But they'll only drift over again," Chet complained.

"Be that as it may," Grandma replied, "if we don't keep up with the drifts, we'll soon be buried in them up to our eyeballs."

"It'd also be nice to be able to get out of the driveway if we need to," Grandpa added. "We don't have any snowmobiles like J. J. or some of our other neighbors do."

Chet flexed his muscles. "Sure thing, Grandma and Grandpa," he said. "If the snow needs clearing, I'm up to it."

"I'm wishing now that we'd bought one of those small, truck-mounted plows from that Sanchez woman," Grandma admitted.

"We'll get by," said Grandpa. "We don't get a blow like this more than once every twenty years or so. By the time the next one comes, we'll be retired and loungin' on that beach where our kids are right now."

The Hardys went and patched the barn wall under Grandpa's direction while Chet cleared the driveway. The repairs were more difficult without power tools, but Mr. Morton still had plenty of old-fashioned woodworking implements lying around the barn, in addition to the boards they needed for the patch.

Iola helped Grandma with the household chores. Then the boys carried in enough wood to last them for the night.

By mid-afternoon, they all had some free time, so the teenagers went outside and built snowmen and a snow fort while the Morton grandparents napped. After a snow fight, the teens happily sipped hot chocolate while sitting around the fireplace and recounting tales of their exploits.

"Maybe those snowmen we built will scare off the prowlers," Chet speculated. "In the dark, they might look like sentries."

"They'd look more like guards if you hadn't been plunking them with snowballs," Iola noted. "Now they'll only work if the burglars think we've hired the Big-Puff Marshmallow Men to guard our house."

"Or that TV salesman guy who's made out of car tires," Joe added, laughing.

"Fear me! I am the amazing blubber man!" Frank said. He lumbered across the room, imitating a walking snowman.

"Okay, so maybe that won't work," Chet admitted.

"I doubt these felons would be frightened off by a scarecrow anyway, Chet," Iola said. "After all, Bernie didn't chase them away, and he's a pretty good watchdog."

"I've been thinking about that," Joe said. "I'm wondering if maybe someone fed Bernie some drugged food."

"That occurred to me, too," Frank said. "You remember how sleepy he was the night someone was skulking outside? And then he got taken away with no signs of a struggle."

"None we could find," Chet said.

"Either he was drugged, or he got nabbed by someone he knew and trusted," Joe said.

"That makes sense," said Iola. "But who?"

The Hardys shrugged. "Joe and I are still working on it," Frank replied.

Dinner time soon rolled around, and their supply of water had already run low.

"Why don't you fetch enough from the water tower to last the night," Grandma suggested.

All four teens groaned. They were starting to feel the aches of all the work and play that day.

"Count your blessings," Grandpa Morton said. "If it weren't for that water tower, we'd either have to melt snow to get water, or you'd have to pump it out by the animal stalls and haul it in from the barn. That'd be almost double the work."

"I suppose we should be thankful that the big tank isn't frozen, too," Iola said.

"That foam insulation in the tank usually keeps it usable," Grandma said, "so there should be enough in there to last us a while. I'm just glad we didn't empty it for the winter like we usually do."

"I have to admit," Grandpa said, "I just plain forgot. It turns out to be a blessing in disguise, though."

"Too bad we can't just run that old firehose up to the house," Frank said.

"The hose is pretty frozen from the other night," Grandpa noted. "You could hit it with a hammer and not bend it. We should probably take it into the barn to thaw out, now that I think of it."

"I don't think that old hose is very sanitary, anyway," Grandma added. "I certainly wouldn't want to drink out of it."

"C'mon, gang," Joe said. "It'll go faster if we form a bucket brigade." He rose and headed for the back hall.

"Sounds like a plan," Frank agreed. He, Chet, and Iola followed.

Their snowsuits hadn't completely dried yet after the snowfight, so they were all a little damp and miserable as they trudged outside.

Chet shook his head. "Look at this," he said, gazing at the drifts covering the driveway. "I'll have to blow it all clean again tomorrow morning."

"Maybe they'll get the phones fixed and be able to call for a plow," Iola said.

"Let's hope," Chet replied. "I think J. J. usually clears out their driveway during the big blows. And he's welcome to the job."

They all went to the water tower to fill up their buckets once. After that, they planned to form a line back to the house and pass the buckets along as they filled them.

Chet had the most experience with the temperamental spigot at the tower's base, so he was elected to be the main bucket filler. "I always did want to find a vocation," he joked as he fiddled with the ancient valve.

As he began to twist, the tower shook suddenly.

A loud snapping sound filled the air, followed by a tremendous groan.

"Look out!" Frank cried. "The tower's falling!"

12 Water Wonderland

One of the four stout wooden legs holding up the tower buckled, tipping the huge container toward the startled teens. The three remaining legs creaked and protested before they started to snap.

Frank grabbed Chet by the collar and pulled him out of the way. At the same time, Joe put his arms around Iola and thrust both of them to one side.

The four teens scrambled as the huge metal container gave a final groan. Then the legs gave way completely and the whole thing tumbled toward them.

"Jump!" Joe cried.

He and Iola dove to one side, and Frank and Chet leaped toward the other. The tower crashed to the icy ground and burst open, spraying countless

119

gallons of water in every direction. The four friends landed in the snowdrifts to either side of the falling tank.

The horrible sound of rending metal filled the air as the tank caved in at the seams. Its wooden top smashed when it hit the ground, filling the air with fragments of timber. Frank ducked as a big board soared past his head, barely missing Chet.

The icy water hit the teenagers like a tidal wave, drenching everyone right through their parkas. For a moment a huge sloshing sound filled the chilly air. Then the barnyard fell silent.

"Is everyone okay?" Joe asked.

Iola and the rest nodded. "Yes, aside from being soaked to the skin," Chet said.

Frank stood up and shook himself. Droplets of water dripped from his parka as though he were a wet dog. "We were lucky," he said. "If that tower had fallen any more quickly, someone could have been killed."

"I'm wondering why it fell at all," Joe said. He sloshed through the chilly water and drenched snow to the tower's broken base.

"What in tarnation?" Grandpa Morton cried. He and Grandma dashed out of the house, pulling on their coats as they came. The two looked around the scene in disbelief. Sorrow and frustration welled up in their aged eyes.

"It just . . . collapsed," Chet said apologetically.

"It was pretty old, Pa," Grandma Morton said consolingly. "All the snow and wind must have taken a toll on it, especially with it being full and all."

Dave Morton nodded slowly. "Must have," he agreed sadly. "Are any of you young'ns hurt?"

"No, we're all fine," Iola replied.

"Though we're going to need to change our clothes . . . again," Joe added. Already their parkas had begun to freeze up.

"This is gonna make getting water more difficult," Grandpa said. "That old pump in the barn is barely enough to water the animals, and I'm not lookin' forward to meltin' snow on the stove."

"We'll work something out, I'm sure," Grandma said. "I guess all of you best come inside and clean up."

"We'll come inside in a minute, Mrs. Morton," Frank said.

She shrugged. "Suit yourself. I'll get the cocoa brewing and set up the drying rack by the fireplace again."

"I'd best check on the pump near the animals," Grandpa said, "and make sure it's still working. You all watch your step out here. This whole place'll be a skating rink in no time. I suppose I better fetch some road salt after I see to the pump."

The two elder Mortons went about their business, leaving the drenched youngsters alone in the driveway near the shattered tower.

"Why didn't you want to go in right away, Frank?" Iola asked, shivering.

"I need to check something first," Frank replied.

"Yeah, me too," Joe agreed.

The brothers examined the fallen tower's base.

"This pylon didn't just snap," Frank said, running his fingers over the wood. "It was cut!" He pointed to the clean break in one of the four wooden support legs and some sawdust resting on the wet snow beneath it.

"Hey, Frank," Joe said, "what do you make of this?" He was looking at some depressions in the snow nearby. The indentations led from the rear of the tower toward the side of the barn.

"Those look like they might be footprints," Chet blurted.

Frank's brown eyes narrowed. "Yeah. Filled in by blowing snow. Let's follow them."

"D-do you mind if I g-go inside?" Iola asked, her teeth chattering. "You can tell me what you find."

"Of course," Joe replied. "Don't freeze on account of us." Iola went back inside the house while the three boys trudged around to the rear of the barn, following the tracks.

"Well, this confirms it," Frank said, pointing to a longer, wider depression behind the barn. The rut led away from the back of the building toward the woods on the north.

Joe nodded. "The snowmobile gang again."

"They're approaching the property from the north, being sure to keep the barn between themselves and the house—and in doing this, they're blocking our view of them."

"I'll say one thing for these bandits," Chet said, "they're bold."

"And dangerous," Joe added. "Someone could have gotten killed, either in the fire they set or during this water tower collapse."

"But what are they after?" Chet asked.

Frank shook his head. "Not sure. I'm working on it. We need to report this to the police, though."

"Assuming the phones are working again," Joe said.

After changing out of their wet clothes, the teens tried the phones again when they got inside, but they were still out. As they tried to get in touch with the police, the Hardys filled the Mortons in on what they'd found.

"This place could really use that cell tower the mall people are promising," Joe said. The brothers' cell phone still wasn't working either.

"No use worrying when there's no way to change it," Grandma said. "We've survived on our own before, and we will again." She had been puttering around constantly since the teens came inside, bringing the boys soup and hot liquids, fetching blankets, and laying out their clothing to dry.

"I've got a shotgun stashed somewhere in the

attic," Grandpa said. "Maybe it's time I fetched it out."

"I suppose that couldn't hurt," Frank said.

"With Bernie kidnapped, the fire, and now this, there's no telling what these criminals might try next," Iola said.

"They've avoided direct confrontation so far," Joe noted.

"Cowards as well as scoundrels," Grandpa said. "A shotgun's almost too good for them."

"It'll have to do until we can get in touch with the police," Grandma said. "You go fetch it, Pa, but don't load it. We don't need any more accidents around here."

Grandpa nodded his agreement and headed up to the attic.

"Surviving through this weather is tricky enough without saboteurs," Joe said.

For a moment Grandma Morton's brave face slipped. She sat down heavily in a rocking chair near the fire. A far-off, misty look came over her gray eyes. "It's not like the old days," she said. "That's for sure."

"It'll be all right, Grandma," Iola said, giving her a hug.

"Yeah," Joe said, "there are plenty of us to help with the chores. I'm sure we'll have everything ship-shape in no time—even before the power comes back on."

Grandma Morton sniffed back a tear. "I sure hope you're right," she said.

Once the Hardys and their friends dried out, they doubled their efforts to help the Mortons. They tackled all their usual chores and tried to do as many of Grandma and Grandpa Morton's tasks as they could too. They used shovels to clear the slush out of the drive before most of it could freeze, and they used the snowblower to clear away the driveway and paths where there wasn't any ice. Then they took care of the animals, pumped and carried in enough water for the rest of the day, and replenished the supply of firewood.

By the time evening rolled around, all four teens were exhausted. They ate ravenously and then collapsed in front of the fire, soaking in the warmth.

There wasn't any game playing or even much conversation around the fireplace that night. Grandma and Grandpa read by the light of the hurricane lanterns for a while before turning in.

The teens came up with a plan to keep watch throughout the night. They took four shifts, with Joe the last one up. The younger Hardy finally crawled back into bed just before sunrise, when he heard Grandpa puttering around.

Though nothing bad happened during their night vigil, keeping watch had left all the teens even more exhausted. They slept well into the morning the next day.

Joe and Frank woke to the sound of roaring engines. Both of them sat shock upright in their beds.

"The snowmobilers!" Joe said. He and Frank both dashed to the bedroom window, which overlooked the front yard. They didn't see the felons, but rather a big Department of Public Vehicles street plow going north past the farm on Kendall Ridge Road. The south lane of the road seemed to have been plowed already. A green pickup truck with a snowplow attached to the front sat in the Morton's newly cleared driveway.

The brothers recognized the truck as being the one J. J. Zuis had arrived in to help fight the fire. As they watched, a late-model sedan pulled out of the drive and skidded onto Kendall Ridge Road. It turned south, heading back toward Bayport.

"It seems like we've slept through some visitors," Frank said.

"Not only that, but the power's back on," Joe said, pointing to a digital clock on the dresser. "Wasn't that the sedan Patsy Stein drove the other day?"

"I think you're right," Frank said. "I guess she doesn't give up easily."

"Real estate developers seldom do," Joe replied.

"If the lights are on, maybe the phones are

working too," Frank suggested. "Let's get dressed and see if the Mortons have gotten in touch with the police yet."

The brothers showered in shifts, then got dressed and joined the Morton family downstairs around the kitchen table. J. J. Zuis and Bill Backstrom were seated with the Mortons, enjoying breakfast. The enticing scent of freshly cooked bacon and toast filled the air.

"Boy, it sure is good to have the power back on," Chet said, beaming over a heaping plate of bacon and eggs.

"I definitely feel a lot cleaner this morning," Iola agreed. Her freshly washed brunette hair was tied up in a towel on top of her head.

"I hate to eat and run," J. J. said, busing his plates to the sink, "but I need to get back home. I may not have as much to clean up as you do, but you know farming: Every time you take a break, something falls apart. And it's not like I can sell the place to Stein and retire; my farm's on the wrong side of the power lines for her mall project."

He smiled wistfully at the Morton grandparents. Marge and Dave Morton exchanged a sober glance.

"Thanks again for breakfast," J. J. said.

"Thanks for plowing us out," Grandma Morton replied. "That old snowblower of ours was ready to have a heart attack, I think."

"You're welcome," J. J. said, pausing to tip his hat at the door. "Take care now."

As the door closed behind J. J., Bill Backstrom said, "I guess I need to get to work too—make sure the barn's in good shape, in case that storm turns back this way."

"The weatherman said the worst of it was headed out to sea," Iola said.

Backstrom shrugged. "You never know," he said. "It's best to be prepared."

"I'll talk to you later, Bill," Grandpa Morton said as he saw his friend out.

"Seems like you've had a lot of visitors this morning," Frank said.

"People were just checking in," Grandma replied. "Seeing how we weathered the storm, that's all."

"We saw Patsy Stein's car leaving as we got up," Joe said.

Grandpa nodded and took a deep breath. "I need to tell you kids something," he said. "Grandma and I have decided to sell the farm."

13 Sold the Farm

Stunned silence filled the farmhouse kitchen.

"But . . . but . . . ," Chet stammered.

"But why?" Iola said, finishing her brother's thought. "All the years our family has owned this land . . . all the history . . ."

"Sometimes it's best to put the past behind you," Grandma said. "Memories and places aren't more important than people, and Grandpa and I think it's probably time to move on."

"Is this because of the trouble with those snow-mobile bandits?" Chet asked.

"It's not just that," Grandpa said. "We're gettin' older. It's harder and harder to keep up with this place every year."

"We could come out and help more often," Iola

129

offered. "There has to be *something* more that we can do."

"We know you kids have tried your best," Grandpa continued. "You've helped as much as you can. But the work is tiring. Farming isn't what it used to be, with foreign trade and market fluctuations and such. Every year it gets harder to make ends meet."

"There are other options, though," Frank said. "Some farms have gone co-op, or at least part of their land has."

"Organic farming is booming too," Joe said, "especially with concerns about pollution and contamination."

"We're old dogs," Grandma replied. "It's a little late for us to be learning new tricks. The problems these past few days have convinced us of that. We're not as young and flexible as we used to be. It's harder for us to cope with adversity."

Chet was still angry. "I'd hate for you to give up the farm just because of a few criminals," he said. "If you can hang on a little longer, I'm sure that Frank and Joe can figure out who's behind this trouble."

"There's nothing we can do," Grandpa said. "We signed the intent papers when Patsy came by this morning. Rebuilding the damage to the barn and the water tower would be time-consuming and expensive, even with the insurance. Selling is easier all around."

"Did you talk to the police yet?" Frank asked. "It's entirely possible that Stein and her group may be causing the trouble—pressuring you to sell out."

"If we call the police, it may mess up the deal," Grandma said. "Stein doesn't care about a broken water tower or a singed barn like other buyers would."

"She probably doesn't care about the fields or forest, either," Iola said, getting a bit mad herself. "When Stein is done, it'll all just be a huge parking lot."

"There is a common garden in the design for the mall," Grandma replied. "It's guaranteed by their charter."

"But what if Stein's behind all this?" Chet asked. "What if she took Bernie, set the barn on fire, shot at us in the woods, and sabotaged the water tower? You can't just let her get away with it!"

"Chet, we don't know that Patsy and her group has anything to do with our troubles," Grandpa said.

"That's why you should bring in the police," Joe reiterated.

"But if we do, and if suspicion wrongfully falls on Stein's group, that would be the end of the deal," Grandpa replied. "No, it's best just to let this sleeping dog lie."

"But what about Bernie?" Iola asked.

"We have to believe that the police will find him, sooner or later," Grandma said.

"Just how important is your land to this mall deal?" Frank asked.

"Very important," Grandpa Morton said. "I don't think they could proceed without it. When Patsy called this morning, the consortium even upped their offer. But the same goes for some of the other properties in the area—every piece is vital to her plan."

"She still needs to get the Costellos on board," Grandma added. "That spur of land they have that sticks down just north of our land, between the power lines and Myint's old factory, is essential."

Grandpa scratched his head. "Seems like this might be the first time Costello and I ever shared a common interest. If everything goes through, all the land from here to the factory will become part of the mall complex."

"So they'll be digging up that big slope we slid down the other day," Joe said.

"I think they're actually counting on that slope to save them digging," Grandpa replied. "A two-level mall would fit real good, stretching from there to the spot where the factory stands now."

"The mall looked very pretty and modern on the plans she showed us," Grandma said.

"Not as pretty as the forest, I bet," Iola sulked.

"I'm sorry, Iola," Grandma said. "But Grandpa and I have to do what we think is best."

"No one can blame you for that," Frank said. "Come on, guys. The snow's let off, and it's warmer out. Maybe we can drag the buggy out of that pond today."

"Good idea," Grandpa said. "It'll be good exercise, too. Don't worry so much about chores today. With Bill around, I'm sure we can handle things here."

The Hardys and their friends suited up and headed outside. The day was chilly and damp, with the temperatures hovering right around freezing. The late morning sun peeked out from between gray clouds. Occasional flurries drifted through, the snowflakes dancing on gentle breezes.

"I can't believe they've sold the farm!" Chet said as soon as they were behind the barn, out of earshot of the house.

"No matter what they've said," Iola added, "they clearly did this because of the trouble. They've always loved this place. When we got here a few days ago, they were talking about handing it over to the next generation of Mortons one day."

"Patsy Stein sure got what she wanted out of all this," Joe observed.

"Costello could benefit too," Frank said, "especially if he's the last holdout on selling, like your grandparents said. He could ask a pretty penny for that land they want, and Stein's consortium would have to pay."

"Extortion sounds like it'd be up Costello's alley," Iola said.

They trudged across the fields, their boots crunching through the melting snow, until they reached the pond where Frank and Joe had crashed.

The buggy sat with its back end tipped up in the air, its front firmly wedged in newly frozen ice. The warmth of the morning had melted most of the snow off of the vehicle, and the protective tarp remained on the engine.

"If we can drag it out," Frank said, "I should be able to get it started."

The teens had come prepared for the job. They'd brought shovels, a pickax, snowbrushes, and a small portable blowtorch with them. They packed some ropes as well, to assist in pulling the vehicle out, plus a small jar of gas to prime the carburetor and hopefully get the buggy running again.

"I wouldn't mention this when the time comes to renew your driver's license, Frank," Chet joked as they sized up the condition of the vehicle.

Frank smiled. "It's not going on my résumé, either," he replied.

The four friends set to work, the hard labor taking the edge off four days of bad news and frustration.

First they used the shovels to clear the unmelted snow away from the work area. Then they worked on the ice, using the torch to melt through a couple of tricky places.

The sky clouded over and the snow picked up as they worked.

"Just what we need," Chet complained, "more snow."

"I don't think it will last," Iola said. "The weather report said the weather was supposed to get warmer and maybe turn the snow to rain."

"Let's hope we get the buggy out of here before it does," Joe said. "I've had enough ice-cold soakings for one week."

Having chipped the ice away from the chassis, they brushed the remaining snow off, then fastened ropes to the frame to pull the buggy out.

It was back-breaking work, but none of them felt inclined to complain. Each of the four teens harbored the feeling that they deserved this for letting the Morton grandparents down. All of them felt they could have—and should have—done something more.

By the time they hauled the buggy out of the water, they were all tired and drenched with sweat. With a heavy sigh, Joe relit the torch and began melting out the wheel joints and connections. Frank pulled the tarp off the engine and tried to start it. Nothing happened.

"Sitting in the cold for a couple of days can't

have done it any good," he said to the others.

"So, do we stay here and try to fix it, cover it with the tarp again and come back for it later, or what?" Chet asked.

"The weather's not going to get any better," Iola said. Already the drizzle of snow had begun to mix with freezing rain.

"Let's see if we can drag it back," Joe said. He'd finished freeing up the wheels and steering. "Leaving it out in the rain won't help it any."

"I can try to work on the engine as we go," Frank said. "Maybe if I dry it out a bit more, it'll start up."

"Let's hope," Iola said.

They fastened ropes to the front for Joe and Chet to pull. Iola pushed on the frame at the driver's side, so she could reach in and steer when necessary. Frank pushed from the rear while at the same time trying to dry off the wet engine parts with some rags they had brought with them.

It turned out that dragging the buggy across the snow wasn't much easier than pulling it out of the pond. They took frequent breaks, especially as the weather worsened. Soon more rain than snow was falling, and the drifts around them were turning into slush. As they all paused to catch their breath, Joe turned his head toward the distant outline of the pine forest.

"What is it?" Frank asked.

"I hear something," Joe said, listening closely.

"Snowmobiles!" Iola gasped.

Sure enough, the faraway whine of small, powerful engines echoed across the snow.

Joe jumped into the buggy's driver's seat. "Prime that carburetor, Frank," he said. "Time to see if all that work you've been doing has paid off."

Frank got their small jar of gasoline from his pocket and put some in the carburetor. Joe turned the key and pumped the gas pedal.

With a sputter and a cough, the old VW engine roared to life.

Chet and Iola cheered.

Frank hopped into the passenger seat beside his brother. "Chet, you and Iola go home and call the cops," he said. "Joe and I will see if we can catch the snowmobilers."

"Check," Chet replied.

"It'll take us about fifteen minutes to walk home," Iola said. "We'll get the police here as quickly as we can. Be careful."

"We will," Joe said.

"And don't drive into any more ponds," Chet cautioned.

"Don't worry," Joe said. "We won't."

He turned the buggy toward the forest and stepped on the gas.

14 Double Snow-Cross

Frank held on tight as Joe gunned the engine and roared away across the snowy field. Chet and Iola soon disappeared from view as the Hardys careened over drifts and between the trees that punctuated the broad pasture.

"We'll have to stop to get a bearing on them," Frank said. "I can't hear the snowmobiles over the buggy's engine."

"I agree," Joe said, "but let's get to the forest first."

They skidded through the field toward the rapidly approaching line of pine trees. Several times Joe skidded the buggy sideways to avoid ponds that had been hidden by drifts. "Boy," he said, "this is hard enough in the day time. I see why you had trouble at night during a snowstorm."

"It'd help if we knew the area better," Frank said, "like those bandits apparently do."

"You're thinking they must be locals," Joe said, "not hired guns—like Stein's assistants."

"Yeah."

"We'll find out soon enough." Joe cut the wheel and they plunged between two big pine trees and into the eastern spur of the forest. Flying through the woods, they soon reached a fork in the snow-covered trail. They knew from the day they'd been caught in the avalanche that one way led to the power lines, and the other toward the old factory.

Joe switched off the motor and both brothers listened.

"The power lines," Frank said.

"Definitely," Joe agreed.

He turned on the engine and veered left, heading north toward the power lines and Vic Costello's farm. The trees whizzed by on either side of the trail—tall, red-barked poles sticking up out of the snow. The buggy plowed through several drifts that had blown across the road.

Once, they went into a skid, but Joe handled it expertly, turning into the swerve and then recovering. A tree zoomed by Frank's side of the car, so close that the elder Hardy could have reached out and touched it.

"That was close," he said.

"I don't think we'll mention that one to Iola," Joe said with a grin.

They broke out of the trees considerably to the east of where they'd run into Costello's dogs. The huge metal electric towers strode like giants across the snowy landscape. More forest lay across the right-of-way to the north, Vic Costello's land. The precipitation had turned completely to rain. Curls of cold mist rose from the drifts where water met snow. The area beneath the power lines looked like a river of slush.

Joe brought the buggy to a halt, switched off the engine, and both brothers listened again.

As they did, two snowmobiles crested a rise to the west and roared past. A big sleek, black machine came first. A smaller, red snowmobile trailed close behind. The two of them rocketed past the Hardys, following the service road.

"Let's get them!" Frank said.

Joe turned the key, but nothing happened. The buggy sat still at the edge of the forest.

Frank unbuckled his seatbelt, ran to the back of the vehicle, and took the jar of gasoline from his pocket. There wasn't much left—enough, he hoped, to start the engine one more time. He primed the carburetor and crossed his fingers.

Joe cranked the starter and the old VW engine roared to life once again.

"Move it!" Frank said, hopping back in and buckling up.

Joe stepped on the gas, and the buggy leaped onto the road. The trail led down the northern side of the swath, running beside the huge power towers, rather than directly beneath them.

The snowmobiles had built up a considerable lead while the buggy was stalled. But even with the rolling terrain beneath the electric lines, the criminals weren't far enough ahead for the Hardys to lose them. Every time the brothers went down a dip they temporarily lost sight of their quarry. Every time they crested a rise, they found them again.

"Keep an eye peeled, in case they veer off the trail," Frank said.

"Sure thing," Joe replied. The buggy began gaining speed.

The snowmobiles seemed to notice the Hardys and began swerving back and forth between the towers. Their tactic didn't work, though. Keeping to the road, the Hardys steadily gained ground on their quarry.

As the buggy drew closer, the red snowmobile pulled up next to the black one. The black rider swerved, nearly crashing his machine into the smaller red vehicle.

"What are they doing?" Joe asked.

The red snowmobile swerved, avoiding the other one. He gunned his throttle and pulled up alongside the black rider. The red driver reached out, seemingly trying to grab the controls of the black machine.

The black driver fought back, pushing the red rider's hands away. The red driver reached for a rifle strapped on the black-helmeted snowmobiler's back.

The black vehicle swerved and its rider pulled his leg out of the way as the two snowmobiles smacked against one another. The black rider kept going, thrusting the red vehicle toward one of the big electric towers.

The red snowmobile turned right, weaving between the tall metal legs. He hit a wet snowdrift on the far side of the tower and lost control. His snowmobile skidded back across the road, directly in front of the Hardys.

Joe cut the wheel to the right, then left again, barely avoiding both the onrushing vehicle and the tower's metal leg.

The red snowmobile crossed the road and nosed down into a dip. He skidded up a rise and the vehicle launched itself into the air. The driver lost his grip on the handlebars as the snowmobile flipped over in midair. Rider and machine soared in two different directions.

The snowmobile crashed into a nearby snowbank. The helmeted man landed hard in a pile of ice and slush at the edge of the woods. He lay flat on his back, motionless.

The black snowmobiler continued down the trail next to the power line, rapidly pulling away from his fallen compatriot.

Joe skidded the buggy to a halt and turned it around. He backtracked down the trail and pulled the buggy to a stop next to the injured man. He and Frank hopped out, though they left the stripped-down VW's engine running. They moved quickly to the side of the fallen man. Fortunately both brothers had first aid training.

"I hate letting that villain go," Joe said, glancing at the black snowmobile as it sped away.

"Saving this guy's life is more important," Frank replied. "He'll probably be able to tell us the identity of the other driver." He studied the man lying in the snow for a few moments, then said, "I don't see anything broken, but his helmet's face plate is smashed."

"We should take the helmet off," Joe concluded, "and see if he's hurt underneath." He grimaced. "Now would be a great time for the cell phone to start working."

"With these electric towers overhead?" Frank said. "Not a chance."

The brothers cautiously removed the red rider's helmet.

Joe nodded slowly when he saw the man's identity. "Elan Costello."

"This is starting to make sense," Frank said.

"You think so?" Joe asked. "I was pretty certain he and his father were on those snowmobiles. But why would Vic Costello cause his own kid to crash?"

"He wouldn't," Frank replied. "If you remember the other night, the bandits had two *black* snowmobiles. Not a black one and a red one."

Joe snapped his fingers. "You're right! So Vic Costello's story about his dogs getting set loose *wasn't* just a ploy."

"No," Frank said. "Someone really did let them out—someone who had something to gain by pressuring both the Costellos and the Mortons."

"And I suddenly have a pretty good idea who that person might be," Joe said.

As the words left his lips, a deafening roar filled the rain-soaked air.

The black snowmobile barreled over a nearby rise, heading straight toward them. The snowmobile driver swiftly leveled his rifle and fired.

15 Power Play

The shot screamed through the soggy air and burst into a nearby snow bank.

"No time to worry about Costello's injuries," Frank said. "Get him into the buggy or we're all dead!"

He and Joe lifted Elan Costello and hustled him onto the back seat of the buggy. As they strapped him down with the seat belts, another shot whizzed by. This one clanked off the leg of the electric tower next to them.

The rain was getting worse, and both brothers nearly slipped as they hurried back into their seats. Joe spun the wheel and gunned the engine. The buggy raced west, away from the oncoming gunman.

Freezing slush flew up from their tires as they went. They hit an icy patch on the trail and nearly skidded out of control. The gunman kept moving toward them, the report of his rifle barely audible over the roar of the buggy's engine.

Chilling, bitter rain drove down around them, stinging their exposed faces and drenching their parkas.

"If we keep this up," Joe said flippantly, "we'll be soaked to the skin again."

"Any time you see some sniper-proof shelter, I'm willing to stop and take it," Frank replied. "Until then, let's keep driving."

The snowmobile pulled closer and fired a shot across the buggy's rear.

Joe cut the vehicle to the left, taking a daring chance and darting between two of the big towers. He wheeled the buggy, spinning it one hundred and eighty degrees around. Then he got back on the service road behind their attacker, who was still going in the other direction.

"Good move, Joe!" Frank said as they headed east again, toward the old factory complex.

"That may have bought us some time," Joe said, "but I don't know that we'll be able to keep ahead of him much longer."

"If we can reach the factory parking lot, we should be able to cut over to the road," Frank said. "On pavement, we could outdistance that sniper easily."

"Of course, this baby isn't street legal," Joe noted.

"It's not legal to shoot at people, either," Frank

replied. "If we get to the street and he follows us, the sniper will have more to worry about than we do."

While the brothers talked, they had increased the distance between themselves and the gunman. Joe's sudden turn had caught the sniper completely off-guard. The criminal nearly spun out as he wheeled his black snowmobile and resumed the chase.

Joe put the pedal to the metal. The buggy bounded over the dips and bumps of the power line service road, going airborne for a few seconds after cresting each rise. The younger Hardy fought to control the modified car chassis, while at the same time trying to maintain their distance from the gunman.

Rain and wet snow splashed all around them, splattering their parkas and their exposed faces. "How's Costello doing in back?" Joe asked.

Frank turned and checked. "He seems okay," he replied. "It's a good thing we strapped him in good."

Crack!

Another shot whizzed past Frank and Joe as the snowmobile marksman found his range once more.

"His shots are getting closer," Frank noted. "He's gaining on us, too."

"I know," Joe replied. "This buggy may be good in the snow, but it's not nearly as good as a snowmobile."

With each passing second, the pursuing sniper closed the distance between the two vehicles.

"Hang on," Joe said. "I'm going to try something."

Frank gripped the side of the buggy's roll-cage, bracing himself.

Joe swerved, taking the buggy off of the roadway and between two of the huge electrical towers. The snowmobiler followed, firing again as he came. Joe cut back in the other direction, weaving between the power scaffolds like a skier running a slalom course.

The sniper kept after him, but all the swerving was throwing off his aim. His shots flew wildly through the air, some ricocheting off of the big metal towers.

"Keep it up, Joe!" Frank said. "I can see the factory ahead, and the road leading out of it looks clear."

"If we can hit the highway, this guy will eat our slush," Joe replied. He splashed the buggy through a huge puddle at a dip in the road, then turned to dart between the towers again.

Crack!

A shot sailed over the brothers' heads and struck a tower ahead of them. It hit one of the connections that held the power lines to the huge metal structure. The line snapped in a shower of sparks and swooped down directly at the buggy.

"Look out!" Frank yelled, but Joe was already swerving. He cut to the left and the electrified line barely missed them. It fell into the wide puddle the brothers had just crossed.

The sniper's black snowmobile hit the puddle

and electricity shot through it. A sound like thunder echoed above the rainstorm. The gunman went rigid and lost his grip as his snowmobile bounded through the electrified puddle and soared up into the air. The gunman's hands flew open convulsively. His rifle arced through the rain and landed at the base of one of the towers. The snowmobile exploded in midair, shattering into a hundred pieces.

The gunman flew head over heels and smashed hard into an icy snowdrift. He didn't get up.

"Yeow!" Frank said.

"Ouch!" Joe agreed. He skidded the buggy to a halt and looked back over his shoulder.

The burning wreckage of the snowmobile covered the slush at the base of one of the big metal towers. The sniper lay motionless in the snow bank nearby.

"I suppose we have to go back and get him medical attention," Joe said.

"I guess we do," Frank replied. "Just be sure to skirt that puddle as we go. The power probably cut out at a substation by now, but just in case . . ."

"Yeah," Joe said. "We don't want to join that guy in the emergency room."

Joe drove back cautiously to where the gunman lay, and both brothers got out of the buggy. "Let's put him in back with Costello," Joe said. "We'll take them to the old factory and call for help."

"This guy should be right at home there," Frank said, lugging the gunman into the back seat. "After all, he owns the place." He took off the sniper's helmet, revealing the unconscious face of Leo Myint.

"Let's hope he's got a first-aid kit somewhere in that factory," Joe said. "He's going to need it."

After making sure both of their passengers would survive the trip, the brothers drove to the factory. When they arrived, they found a second black snowmobile parked outside the back door.

Just then, the door opened and a young man with a snowmobile helmet in his hand came out. Seeing the Hardys next to his vehicle, he charged.

Frank dropped and swept out the attacker's knees with a martial art's kick. At the same time, Joe stepped forward and planted a solid right uppercut to the man's jaw. The snowmobiler's head snapped back, and he went out like a light.

"Who is this guy?" Joe said, looking at their unconscious assailant. "I don't think we've ever seen him before."

"He must be one of Myint's workers," Frank replied. "A 'hired gun' who was in on the scheme with his boss."

"So he's the second guy we fought in the barn that night," Joe deduced.

The brothers dragged the bad guys inside and tied them up. They brought Elan Costello in and laid him on a couch in Myint's reception area, then they found a working phone and called the police and an ambulance.

Dark shadows crowded the old factory's interior. All the power seemed to be out, probably because of the broken line. In the darkness the brothers heard something that made them smile. Joe produced his recharged penlight from his coat pocket, and the two of them did some exploring. In a back corner of the factory, near the restrooms, they found a huddled, shaggy shape chained to a wall: Bernie, the Mortons' missing dog.

Bernie looked hungry and tired, but not mistreated. He jumped up and barked excitedly when he spotted the brothers.

After turning Myint and his accomplice over to the police, the Hardys and the Mortons gathered in the kitchen of the old family farmhouse. The brothers' experience with the power lines had left the whole area temporarily without electricity, but all of them had gotten used to living by lamplight anyway. Bernie seemed almost as glad to be home as the Mortons were glad to have him back.

"Leo Myint!" Grandpa Morton exclaimed. "He was causing all the problems? What did *we* ever do to *him*? We've only met the man a couple of times in all the years he's owned that old factory."

"Yes," Grandma Morton said. "Why was he giving us so much trouble?"

"It wasn't just you," Frank explained "He was out to get anyone in his way—anyone who stood between him and what he really wanted: the sale of his factory to Patsy Stein's mall consortium."

"Myint's business was failing," Joe said. "He had bought the old factory complex years ago, but it was more space than he could use. He could never rent out enough of it to cover his costs. Once his business hit the skids, he needed a way out."

"Due to the rough economy, buyers for a factory complex like that are few and far between," Frank said. "The police told us he'd had the place up for sale for three years. Stein was his only hope to get out before he lost his shirt."

"There was a problem, though," Joe said, "Stein didn't want his land unless she could have yours, and a piece of Vic Costello's farm as well."

"So Myint figured if he could give Grandma and Grandpa enough trouble, they'd sell out," Iola concluded.

"That's about the size of it," Frank said. "Myint got one of his factory workers to help him in the sabotage. Working together, they caused a lot of trouble."

"Those scoundrels!" Grandpa said. "It makes me wish I was younger so I could give them a good thrashing. And their scheme nearly worked, too!"

"What do you mean *nearly*?" Chet asked.

"We got a call from Patsy Stein a couple of minutes ago," Grandma Morton explained. "She and her group are backing out of their offer. They don't need the bad publicity associated with Myint's crimes. Plus, Costello has refused to sell them that spur he owns by the factory. Without that little piece of Costello's land, the mall project can't go forward."

"First time Vic Costello has ever done *us* a favor," Grandpa said. "We owe him one."

"Myint harassed Costello, too," Frank said. "He let loose their dogs and tried to pull the same kind of sabotage that he pulled on your place." The elder Hardy reached down and ruffled Bernie's shaggy head. Bernie woofed appreciatively.

"But Elan Costello almost caught Myint today," Joe said. "Elan got on his snowmobile and chased Myint into the woods by the power lines. Lucky for us he did, or we might never have bagged that villain."

"Not too lucky for Elan, though," Chet noted. "How long did they say he'd be in the hospital?"

"He didn't have any broken bones," Joe replied, "just a concussion."

"The doctors are keeping him overnight for observation," Frank said. "He should be fine, though."

Grandma Morton shook her head and sighed. "It's ironic," she said. "If we'd talked to Costello more, we might have noticed the criminals' pattern and figured out that someone was out to drive us both off our land. Oh, well! We've got time to make amends. Even neighbors who haven't been friendly in the past can learn to live with each other in the future."

"So, you're keeping the farm?" Iola asked, hope brimming in her gray eyes.

"Yep," Grandpa replied. "It was a mistake agreeing to sell in the first place. We were just worn out when we agreed to it."

"We're not city people," Grandma added. "We're farm folk. Retirement's not for us. Not yet, anyway."

"That's great!" Chet blurted. "We'll come back next summer and help out for sure."

"Count us in, too," Frank said.

Iola smiled. "Now the Morton farm can stay in the family for another five generations."

"And much of the thanks goes to you, Frank and Joe," Grandpa said.

The brothers smiled at their friends.

"We were lucky," Joe concluded. "If things had gone wrong, it would have been us who'd have bought the farm!"